The Prince With No Heart

EMMA HOLLY

The Prince with No Heart

E nter the magical kingdom of Madrigar, where handsome Prince Augustin was robbed of his heart by a cruel fairy. Blessed by a kinder member of the fae with an "untiring" sword, he's learned such gifts present challenges—and that missing hearts are no light burden.

Plucky Princess Violet likewise suffers under a spell, fated to burn forever with desires no common lover can satisfy. Little do they know the survival of both their kingdoms depends on them losing their enchanted hearts to each other.

*A **very** grownup fairytale from Emma Holly*

"I am utterly insane for Emma Holly. The way she sucks you into her world is pure genius!"
—*New York Times* bestseller, **Jacquelyn Frank**

Chapter 1

Once upon a time, in the realm of the Scarlet Queen, a prince was born with no heart.

In every other respect he was healthy, adorable even, with a duck-like tuft of golden hair and eyes as deeply blue as a summer sky. Sadly, his mother had offended a powerful fairy, and this had caused her son to be cursed. The fairy Gratiana was famous for her pride. She did not forgive insults, even accidental ones. Horrified by her spite and moved by the mother's tears, a much kinder fairy named Ariel pronounced a blessing over the bassinet.

Ariel's words were as generous as the first fairy's had been cruel.

"I bless this boy," she pronounced as the swaddled infant stared up at her, wide-eyed as a little owl.

"Augustin," whispered his mother. No fool, Queen Isabella knew the use of her baby's name would make the fairy's magic more powerful.

"I bless this *Augustin*," Ariel said, though she didn't like being corrected any more than her rival. "Great beauty shall he possess, and even greater vitality. No weapon forged by man or fae shall harm him, so long as he honors me, his godmother."

"Nicely put!" exclaimed her husband. Clevis was a handsome man, but not the brightest star in the firmament. "I want to give the lad a blessing too. Beauty is hardly enough to bring a man happiness. I say this Augustin's sword should be untiring, and make all the ladies swoon . . . you know, once he grows up and all."

"You honor me," the queen murmured, curtseying deeply to them both. Having learned her lesson with Gratiana, she did not question—except perhaps privately—whether this second gift was appropriate.

Thus was Prince Augustin cursed and then charmed from an early age.

Chapter 2

P rince Augustin loved his life, or thought he did anyway. Having been born without a heart, it could be difficult to say. What did other people mean by *love*? Was it deeper than his emotions? Did it bring them more joy? From what he could tell, love brought most people who felt it pain. He didn't see why *he* should go into decline because some laundress he fancied had married another man. Weren't there multitudes of laundresses in the world? And didn't most of them desire him?

One thing he knew for certain: It was good to be him.

On this particular fine spring morning, he was on his way to the scullery. Thanks to the fairy Clevis's blessing, he'd begun the day with his usual immense cockstand. Because he honestly wasn't capable of waiting, he'd worked himself to release by grinding against one of the pillows he'd learned from experience to keep close. He often awakened in the middle of the night to find a down-stuffed square clamped between his thighs, his desperate prick humping it . . . sometimes for the second time.

Even in sleep, Augustin was randy.

This morning, the pillow had tided him over until the pretty maid who brought his breakfast tray arrived. Ravenous, he'd fallen on her, with mutually pleasurable results. Once she recovered from her orgasmic swoon, she'd expressed appreciation for his vigor. That had led to another round of thumping her bottom into his mattress as she alternately giggled and sighed with bliss. He'd roared out his satisfaction as his cock exploded, only just remembering to pull out and spend on her belly.

Naturally, this hadn't exhausted him. His sword was "untiring," after all. His morning wash was all it took to refresh him, after which he dressed in casual buckskin pants and a hunting shirt. Prepared to enjoy his day, he was jogging down the stone-lined spiral of the back stairs. A new scullery maid had recently joined the staff, cute as a button and shyly flirtatious. The memory of how she'd blushed when he'd smiled at her the other day had his cock nudging up in his underclothes.

Surely nothing could be better than tupping a new woman for the first time.

To his dismay, when he reached the castle's cavernous kitchen, it was not the kindly cook who awaited him.

A tall, regal-looking woman rose from behind a heavy plank table. Her braided golden hair was touched by silver, but her fair skin remained unlined. A gown of deep blue velvet skimmed her admirable figure, the rich fabric slashed on the upper part of the sleeves to allow ruches of snow white silk to peep through. From the satin ribbons that bound her beneath her breasts, her long skirts fell gracefully. Though she was both female and beautiful, the prince's cock wilted.

"Mother," he said, offering her a respectful bow.

"Augustin," she returned sternly.

He straightened warily. Of all the inhabitants of the castle, only Queen Isabella refrained from coddling him. "You shouldn't be here," he said. "Your slippers will get dirty in these old rushes."

"Would that I had a choice. My only son so skillfully avoids me I must lay in wait for him wherever he's likeliest to go."

Over by the hearth, the young boy who scraped out ashes emitted a small snigger. He was one of a handful of kitchen servants who were pretending not to eavesdrop.

"Perhaps we shouldn't discuss this here," he said.

"Where then, my darling offspring? Behind the stables? Under the hedge to our peasants' fields? Or perhaps we could speak at the ale house down in the village, where—apparently—all the barmaids like to 'sit on your lap' by turns."

"That isn't—What I mean to say is, we usually move to a darker corner before we start to play in earnest."

"*Usually*," his mother repeated. "How reassuring to know my son isn't *always* making a spectacle of himself."

Augustin's cheeks grew hot, which he did not enjoy at all. He might not possess a heart, but his pride was intact, thank you. A prince ought not to be berated like a child in front of servants.

His mother must have sensed his anger, because she stepped to him and laid cool palms to either side of his face. He was taller than most men, and she had to reach up for this.

"Augustin," she said gently. "You are six and twenty. This has

3

gone on long enough."

"It is my nature. It is how I enjoy my life."

"You need to settle down a *little*. To marry and get an heir."

"My behavior would hurt any wife I took. You always say I should be considerate of others' feelings, even if I can't experience them myself."

His mother searched his eyes, probably trying to puzzle out what was going on behind them. Augustin didn't like when people did this; it made him think they pitied him—poor "Prince No Heart" and rot like that. Out of respect, he stood still for her. After a bit, she dropped her hands from his face and sighed.

"Do you love even me?" she murmured wistfully.

Something stirred inside him, as if an animal were trapped in the place where his heart should have been. Despite the odd physical sensation, his emotions did not alter from mild annoyance—or the vast underlying calm he suspected was emptiness.

"I am what I am," he said.

His mother patted his arm. "You are," she conceded. "And I love you regardless, which is why I ask you to think of your future. Your father and I won't be around forever."

"Can I not marry after you die?"

His mother choked out a laugh, so he supposed this wasn't what he ought to have said. She shook her head and patted him again. "I will settle for your presence at dinner. The King and Queen of Llyr are arriving with their two daughters. Perhaps you'll like one of them."

Liking them wouldn't be the problem. Augustin was attracted to most women, as they were to him. The challenge lay in not sleeping with a female he'd be honor bound to marry.

"The North Road has been beset by a gang of thieves. None of the men from nearby towns have been able to defeat them. Rumor has it the gang could be trolls. The townspeople requested me to act as their champion."

"Tonight?" his mother asked in exasperation.

"It is the dark of the moon. If the thieves are unnatural creatures, their power will be at its ebb. I wouldn't want to miss my best chance to slay them until next month. And you cannot want to leave travelers at their mercy in the meantime."

His mother's brows lowered at his logic. As she well knew, Ariel's blessing uniquely suited him for ridding the land of pests. No weapon forged by man or fae could harm him, and he was very strong. Because she didn't want to admit it, one lovely finger poked his breastbone. "You are too clever for your own good."

"That gift I inherited from you."

She smiled wryly, rising to her toes to press a light kiss upon his cheek. "The princesses are staying for a fortnight. I shan't allow you to evade them indefinitely."

Augustin knew she meant it. Queen Isabella was a woman of her word. Admiration mingled with dismay as he watched her glide out of the kitchen, the same as if it were her queen's chamber. He became aware of bustle increasing around him: Cook and her troops preparing for visitors.

When his wandering eye found hers, Cook looked up from the slab of venison she was noisily cleaving. She smiled at his attention, not too old to be affected by his beauty. The part of him the fairy's husband blessed thought she must have been a comely girl.

"Can't blame a mother for being a mother," she said to him.

"No," he agreed, because how else could he respond? Glumness overtook him like a scudding cloud. He didn't know how much longer he could escape his mother's plan to geld him. Though he wasn't often unhappy, his downturned mouth had its usual effect on Cook.

"New girl is in the pantry," she said. "Perhaps a bit of conversation would cheer you up."

Augustin smiled so brilliantly the woman's mouth fell open in dazzlement.

"You're a queen!" he exclaimed, his prick leaping up in an eager surge. He shook his pants leg to make room for it and strode off, everything and everyone forgotten in the glow of this new prospect.

Unseen behind him, Cook pressed one plump hand to the palpitation in her bosom.

Chapter 3

T he wolf was at Violet's door . . . literally.

Ever since the seal people stole her parents, Princess Violet had been responsible for protecting the tiny—and not particularly wealthy—kingdom of Arnwall. Nearly a thousand souls relied on her for their safety, and who knew how many sheep and goats? She simply couldn't afford to take a misstep now.

She studied her grim reflection in the cheval mirror as her maid fussed over the fall of her pale blue gown. It was unfortunate she was small, or she'd have been considered a greater beauty. That would have been useful for attracting champions and suitors, seeing as her kingdom was no great prize. She consoled herself that her skin was smooth and creamy, her body slender, and her eyes—so she had been told—as green and sparkling as polished peridot. Nice as this was, her hair was by far her best asset. Wavy and thick, the shining locks were the vibrant red of maples in autumn. Rumor had it the Scarlet Queen's ruby hair did not glow so brightly as Violet's. Having never met the high queen, she could not venture to say, though her tresses did hang to her ankles. Even as the seal people's naked king had been carrying her mother into the waves, she'd cried back to Violet that she must not cut it.

That wasn't a request a dutiful daughter could disobey.

Today, she wore her hair tightly braided and bound back with blue ribbons. If she didn't, it caused more trouble than she had patience for. Wishing her current life didn't try her patience, Violet let out a quiet sigh.

"You shouldn't have to meet that man," clucked her maid. Always attentive to detail, Etta pulled a finger's breadth more ruches from the slashes in the upper pouf of Violet's sleeve. "That ruffian isn't fit to breathe the same air as you."

"I'll only make things worse if I refuse to see him," Violet said reasonably. "If he believes he's gaining ground with me, he'll refrain from more attacks."

6

"Sir Catallan could—"

"Sir Catallan served my parents well as an advisor, but he is too old to challenge Bojik in combat. I couldn't bear to lose a faithful friend that way."

Etta frowned, stepping back to survey her work. "The men of this land are cowards."

"They aren't cowards. They simply value their lives. Bojik is as bloodthirsty as he is ruthless. Add to that his were-wolf strength, and he's well nigh unstoppable."

"Your honor deserves to be defended! If your blessed father knew how his knights had failed you, he'd thrash every one of their bottoms red."

Heart overflowing, Violet turned and kissed the cheek of her staunchest champion. "You defend me, Etta. That's all I need to sustain my nerve."

"Hmph." The maid wiped angry tears from her eyes. "You have the charm bag I gave you?"

"Right here," Violet assured her, patting her pale blue bodice.

She didn't tell her beloved servant that the magical protection wasn't helping. The fire Bojik had cursed her with burned inside her without surcease. Unaware that he was witch as well as were-wolf, she'd laughed at him when he first started pursuing her. No princess would roll in the hay with a commoner, even if he didn't turn into a ravening beast every month. Bojik had been more lovesick than she'd comprehended, because next he'd offered to wed her. She'd laughed at that too, a memory that pricked her with shame today.

Enraged and mortally insulted, Bojik had snatched a single strand of hair from her head, vowing she'd beg him to swive her before the cock's next crow. Surely enough, the following morning she'd woken with a lust bigger than the moon flaming and creaming within her sex. Pleasuring herself had not eased it, nor did the fever ever completely go away. Her nipples were tight as stones as she strode down the wooden corridor toward her enemy. The constant fluttering in her swollen pearl grew stronger with every step, the swish of her layered gown a tease against her legs. The coolness of the air on her cheeks informed her she was flushing.

Her blood knew she could get what it wanted. She only had to weaken.

If her mother had been around to witness how she'd brought this torment upon herself, Violet knew she'd have commanded her to apologize to Bojik. Arnwall's queen had been a light of kindness and compassion to all she met. Violet had many leagues to go before she could fill her slippers.

Her only consolation was that she doubted an apology would have helped.

The were-witch Bojik awaited Violet in the great hall. The large space was built of wood, and had withstood the march of two centuries. To her who had been born here, the arching wings of the ceiling trusses were the most beautiful in the world. The tapestries of hunting scenes were frayed but lovely, the black oak floors neatly swept. Her people might be poor, but they took pride in this place they lived.

When Violet had approached close enough to speak to, Bojik drew a bouquet of wildflowers from behind his back.

"Violets for my Violet," he said.

In that moment, she wished she could love him. If she had, perhaps she could have tamed his violence. She could not doubt his feelings for her ran deep. His hope that she would return them was as obvious as the crooked smirk that hid it.

Accept him, her inflamed body urged. *This suffering can end today.*

She touched her bodice and remembered the terror his acts had struck in her people. Shielding them was her duty. She could not give this monster more power by making him their king.

"Thank you," she said, taking the flowers from him. "I believe I saw a pitcher of water left on the high table."

They walked side by side, unspeaking, down the length of the soaring room. Bojik was a young man, handsome in his rough way. His brown hair was shaggy, his eyes as dark as wet bark. His jaw was strong, and likewise his broad shoulders, which were pulled straight due to him clasping both hands behind his back. He was more than tall enough for her, though not as tall as men got. The thick muscles of his thighs looked like they could pump his rampant phallus into a girl for hours.

Stop it, Violet ordered, wrenching her gaze from the swiftly expanding bulge it had drifted to. Sadly, she was too late. The image was already burned in her brain, the soft chamois cloth so snug around his penis she had no trouble seeing it in detail. The bulbous head was caught in his trouser leg, its size truly marvelous. Sweat broke out on her forehead, the pain between her legs savage.

"Here we are," she said a trifle hoarsely, pouring water from the pewter pitcher into a wooden cup. "I hope your flowers don't get drunk from the dregs of wine in this."

"Violet," he groaned, having heard what was in her voice. Seizing her trembling hand, he pulled it to his flat stomach. His cock was an inch away, its heat beating strongly against her wrist.

Violet flattened her other hand on his broad hard chest. "You and I must talk."

"All you ever want to do is talk. Don't you know how wonderful you would feel if you gave in to me? We could stay in bed for days, tupping around the clock. My beastly cock is what you need, Princess. No other man can sate the terrible itch in you."

"Because of you! You cursed me to want you."

Bojik smiled, his dark eyes sliding in a hot caress to her tight nipples. "I cursed you to want, Violet. That you want *me* is your own weakness."

Her anger lent her the power to fling away. "Why do men think wanting is enough?"

"It is *not* enough, but it will do for a start."

His voice was hard, the hurt in it muted. She refused to weaken just because he had real feelings. She crossed her arms over her pulsing breasts. "My tenants lost more sheep during the last full moon."

"And you assume that is on my head?"

"The animals' bellies were torn out and their hearts eaten. No other predator leaves beasts thus."

She did not quail at his narrowed gaze, nor he at her accusation. "My wolf does what it does. I cannot be held responsible."

"You are your wolf! If you have no control, why are *your* flocks not waning? Or are your sheep not as tasty as other men's?"

She had pushed him too far with this, though every word was true. His hands made fists by his sides, his face reddening with temper.

"You are a woman," he said between clenched jaws. "And women have tender hearts. For the sake of this, I wrestle with my wolf's hunger for human flesh. Do not mistake my restraint for handing you the power to turn me into a lapdog."

"I don't want to turn you into anything. I want you to leave me and my folk alone!"

Fire flashed from Bojik's eyes. Grabbing her by the shoulders, he hauled her onto her toes mere inches from his body. She tried to struggle, but his strength was greater than an ordinary man's. Annoyed by her resistance, Bojik shook her like a child.

"No!" she insisted, slamming her knee into the one spot all men were vulnerable.

Bojik cursed but did not release her. He forced her back until she lay on the scarred old planks of the high table, her long red braid spilling to the side. One iron hand was all he needed to manacle her wrists. With them stretched above her head, he had no trouble pushing up her skirts. Tremors ran along her thighs as a draft blew through her flimsy drawers.

"We are made for each other," he said. "How long will it take you to see that?"

He made a low pained sound as his groin notched hers, his powerful body spreading her helpless legs. Violet bit her lip to keep her own moan inside. As he rocked his cock hard against her, grunting with his pleasure, the fluid that had been gathering inside her spilled out in a hot rush.

So generous a flood could not be overlooked. Bojik groaned, his mouth crashing down on hers.

Madness overtook her at the forceful thrust of his tongue. He felt so good hitching tight to her sex, far better than her fingers or any of the toys she'd resorted to lately. Kissing him back, she writhed under him, desperate to rub herself against him as vigorously as he rubbed her. She wanted to embrace him, but he held her wrists captive. Forced to urge him by other means, she sucked his tongue more strongly into her mouth.

He gasped for air, his free hand working eagerly into the slit of her linen drawers. She groaned as he found her pussy, her wetness coating his entire palm. He twitched in reaction, and panted, and slid the tip of one finger past the wild throb of her entrance.

"This is mine," he hissed, pressing her maidenhead. "My prick shall breach it, and you *will* have to marry me."

Though he kissed her again at once, her mind momentarily cleared. *What am I doing?* she thought. *How did he push me into losing control this fast?* With a heroic effort, she tore her starving lips from his.

"No," she said as firmly as she could. "I do not give you permission to take me."

He gaped at her in disbelief, his chest heaving raggedly. For a moment, she thought he'd ravish her anyway. Slowly he released her arms and pushed back from her. She sat up to chafe the bruises blooming around her wrists, her limbs shaking violently. Her reaction wasn't fear of him so much as shock at herself. If he'd pressed her two heartbeats longer, she'd have succumbed.

Perhaps he knew this. Grunting, he dug into his breeches to shift his engorged penis to stand knob up—to make it more comfortable, she supposed. Violet's gaze was glued to his motions, including the pass his thumb made around the crown. The little hole must have been weeping. His thumb came away shining. Bojik brought it to his mouth and sucked. Despite the horror she should have felt, Violet only ripped her eyes away when his dark chuckle startled her.

"You are not as strong as you think," he mocked. "For now, I accept your answer, but only because this is the last time you'll ever say no to me."

Violet swallowed, unable to say a word. Her pussy swam with fresh moisture, its aching emptiness pure torture. As Bojik left her sitting there with her skirts flung up and her face ablaze, she feared most heartily he spoke true.

Chapter 4

V iolet knew she had little choice. If she stayed in Arnwall, Bojik would seduce her. Perhaps not tomorrow but presumably the day after. Because of her weakness, innocent people would never be free of him.

She crawled out of bed before the sun had risen, careful not to rouse Etta, who slept in an adjoining room. Simply dressed, she packed a handful of belongings and a supply of food. These she tied in a little sack, which she slung over her shoulder.

With these humble preparations, she left to seek her champion.

A tenant's wagon provided concealment for the first leg of her journey down Arnwall's rocky coast. Hidden beneath a tarp with a load of turnips, she was able to travel undetected for many miles. When she saw they'd reached the Wailing Woods, she rolled out silently. Though the forest was reputed to be haunted, its trails would lead her to dragon lands. Those wild and dangerous beasts attracted knights like flies. She hoped to convince one of the braver ones to help her—the sooner, the better. She didn't want to think how Bojik would vent his anger once he discovered she'd run away.

Regretfully, lying still so long among those turnips, unable to make a sound, had caused her cursed arousal to collect viciously.

Her thighs were damp with the slow trickle of her cream, but she forced herself to hike up her skirts and hurry into the forest along the dirt paths she found. She believed she was moving west, though her distraction made it difficult to be sure. Each time her heels struck the earth, the impact sent vibrations running up her leg bones to her pussy. She began to run, hoping perhaps she'd come. To her dismay, she only succeeded in worsening her torture.

She moaned to herself, unable to keep it in. Luckily, no one but forest creatures were there to hear.

A clearing appeared before her, encircled by towering pines. In its center, an ancient fruit tree crouched. Her attention split, Violet cried out as a root tripped her. The fall flung her headlong onto the mossy ground, a foot from the base of the dying tree. A raven the size of a cat squawked in protest, taking flight from the gnarled branches. Violet barely noticed. Her little sack had fallen ahead of her. Her fingers fumbled to untie it.

Hurry, she thought. *Hurry or you'll go mad.*

She fought a knot free and thrust one arm inside. Her lower lip trickled blood where a stone had cut it, and she just didn't care. Her favorite ivory dildo bumped her fingers, the thing so thick and long it had frightened her when she saw it among the peddler's wares. It was lifelike and smooth as satin, with twisting veins carved on its surface. Its bottom flared like a set of ballocks. Its crown, which was slightly wider than Bojik's, dipped inward at its center in a convincing urethra.

She'd known she had to have it, no matter what it cost.

The moment she pulled it free, she rolled onto her back, lifting her hips so she could drag up her gown. She sprawled her knees out without delay. Her drawers had a slit she could reach into. At her absolute limit, she pushed the dildo's head half an inch inside her.

Sometimes she came just from this, but that wasn't the case today. Her body craved full penetration, and that she could not supply. The proof she was a virgin was too valuable to destroy. Crazed with lust, she squirmed wildly around the head. All five fingers of her other hand found occupation over and around her clitoris. Up and down she rubbed, and then in a hard circle. Only this could fend off the temptation to shove the dildo all the way into her.

She groaned as she frigged herself, tugging both pearl and labia as hard and fast as she could. Beams of cathedral light spiked through the evergreen canopy as she thumped her hips on the ground. Despite her efforts, her arousal spiked higher, not breaking into climax as she needed it to do. She was grateful no one could see her, for she would have seemed a soul bedeviled.

"Please," she begged to the sky. "Please, I'll do anything."

Maybe some spirit heard her. The quality of her excitement changed, her arousal gaining momentum in a new way. Grunting, Violet pulled out the dildo and rolled onto her belly. The mossy ground was soft as velvet, its hummocks as firm as a man's body. Knowing she needed more stimulation than her fingers were giving her, she twisted around to press the head of her toy to the pucker that pierced her crack. The dildo was very wet. Her sphincter woke as she pressed it, throbbing fiercely with blood and heat.

"Ah," she cried as she pushed it inward, the fingers on her clitoris moving ever more frantically.

She couldn't reach well enough to push the ivory phallus in all the way, but the best nerves were in the outer reaches of her passage. She jiggled the part of the dildo that resembled a pair of balls. The deepest possible sensations radiated outward from the other end. She was going to come. She could feel the peak rising. She seemed to see a face in her mind—not Bojik's, thank the Lord—but a man's face lowering from a great distance to kiss hers. Her tongue curled out in longing, the blood from her cut lip dripping to the ground. Her sex began to tingle before she could distinguish the man's features.

Her pussy clenched sharply in warning. The climax was upon her, breaking like a hundred bells ringing.

She must have been so maddened she was seeing visions. Light seemed to burst from her in brilliant rays, as if her body had turned into a sun. She groaned, the orgasm so good, so hard she couldn't have remained silent to save her life. It rolled over her in honeyed waves, like bliss or love—though she was alone.

The intensity of the cataclysm exhausted her. Minutes passed before she opened her eyes. Her body was at peace for the first time since Bojik had bespelled her. The dildo had been jostled from her, but she didn't need it now.

A purr of sensual relief trailed pleasurably from her throat. She turned limply onto her back to enjoy her lassitude.

It was then she realized the twisted tree above her was bursting with new green leaves.

Violet sat up amazed. No longer clinging to life, the tree had regained its youth. Every twig was sprouting, every branch cloaked in emerald. Small white flowers twinkled from the foliage, no doubt on their way to fruiting. Violet knew this transformation had to be the result of magic, but who could have performed it?

"My friend would like to thank you," said a gentle, whispery voice.

Violet twisted around to see who'd spoken. A hunched old woman stood an arm's length away on the mossy ground. Her clothes were ragged brown burlap, loose and hooded to cover all of her. Violet should have been afraid or embarrassed, but what she experienced was a deep wonder.

"Are you saying *I* did this?" she asked.

"Pleasure and blood are tried and true offerings. The energy they release can work miracles. You've earned a boon from me for this one—if you wish it."

Violet lost her last doubt that a fairy addressed her. Though a boon would be useful, the fae were notoriously tricky.

"I have need of aid," she confessed, "but I don't know what to ask for. Could I explain my situation and leave the cure to your great wisdom?"

The fairy laughed at her ploy, her voice suddenly younger. "Tell me your troubles, child. I promise my solution will not lead you to misery."

Violet could ask no fairer, so she confided her travails.

"You have my condolences on the loss of your parents," the fairy said, once her tale had concluded. "Stories of their goodness were known even in fae lands."

Violet's throat tightened to hear this. Her parents had indeed been wonderful people.

"Well," said the fairy. "Spilled milk cannot be returned to the cow. We must do what we can with the cup before us."

From the pocket of the dusty rags she wore, she produced a bundle of wrinkled silk. A wave of her hand untied it, revealing three objects. Both Violet and the fairy had sat on the ground while she shared her story. Now Violet leaned over the space between them to see what the old woman had brought out.

On the square of creased brown silk lay a snarl of gray thread, a walnut still in its shell, and a golden bit much too small to fit in a horse's mouth.

The crone laughed softly at her confusion. "Listen closely, young Violet, for a fairy's guidance must be followed to the letter. The land of Madrigar is your destination, beyond the Western brink of the Wailing Wood. There lives a prince by the name of Augustin, and he is your champion."

"Does he know he's my champion?" Violet asked doubtfully.

"Assuredly not." The fairy sounded amused. "Nor would he be eager to come with you if you asked. He has plenty of beasts to battle right where he is. You being a pretty young princess would also do you no favors. Augustin has a horror of well born females."

"Then, if you please, dame, how am I to convince him?"

The fairy nodded in approval of Violet's manners. "First you must disguise yourself. Hide this clump of thread somewhere on your person, and you will immediately be clothed as a beggar girl. Thus garbed, you may proceed to the king's stables, where I chance to know they will need a horse charmer. Murmur 'Violet loves you' into any horse's ear, and the most rambunctious stallion will calm for you."

The fairy continued in this vein with her instructions, requesting Violet to repeat them at intervals. When she was satisfied the princess had them by rote, she retied the bundle of enchanted items and handed them over. Violet accepted it carefully.

"One warning," the fairy added—as fairies were wont to. "The prince suffers from a condition similar to your own. His appetite for coitus cannot be quenched. To make matters worse, the beauty and vitality with which he is blessed guarantee that his seductions are almost impossible to resist. Even direr—" She paused to pin Violet with her gaze. "Even direr, to allow the prince's sword within one's pussy guarantees a woman such flagrant pleasure that she cannot help but swoon as she releases. You must not allow him into that part of your body, no matter how he tempts you. The worst possible madness would overwhelm you both. You would forget your people and your honor to stay with him. As you know, without your protection, great evils will befall your lands."

"I'll do as you say," Violet promised, though in truth she wondered if she'd be able to. The fairy's description of the prince's troubles had her fighting not to squirm in her cross-legged pose. Within her sex, muscles clenched against each other, the flesh they moved tender and swollen. Her cream-drenched pearl felt three times the size it ought to have been.

"See that you keep your promise," the fairy said, rising gracefully despite her hunched appearance. "Of all my instructions, refraining from intercourse with the prince is the most important to follow."

Violet regained her feet awkwardly, remembering to curtsey once she was up.

"Good," said the fairy. "My raven will lead you safely through the forest. Time is of the essence. Do not stop for anything."

Then, before Violet could thank her or ask questions, the fairy vanished into thin air. All that remained of her presence was a slowly descending sparkle of fairy dust.

The fairy's raven, the same bird Violet had startled from the fruit tree, cawed at her as she stood gaping.

"Well." Violet bent to retrieve her things. "I suppose I'd better follow you."

*

Two days later, having been led by the raven through the Wailing Woods, Violet felt like a beggar girl. Magical disguises were not required. They'd traveled without food or rest, and she was dirty from head to toe, her long hair a mess that was more a memory of a braid than the braid itself. She'd walked through the soles of her slippers, her feet stinging now with cuts. She was hungry and tired and one snapped twig away from weeping.

On the bright side, she was too exhausted to be aroused.

When the raven fluttered down to a boulder and cawed at her, Violet plopped next to it.

"This had better be it," she said.

They sat atop a low promontory beneath a dark gray sky. A pre-dawn mist shrouded their surroundings, but she discerned rolling hills. The raven fluffed its wings as she tried to find a comfortable position on the rock. Because it hadn't rested either, Violet poured it a drink from her water bag. The bird dipped its beak and drank, then sidled closer on big black claws, only stopping when it leaned wearily into her side.

Violet laughed and stroked a gentle finger around its glossy head. "Are you a prince then? Enchanted to take bird form by some cruel fairy?"

If it was, it couldn't answer. Instead, it tucked its head low and slept. Violet watched the sunrise alone, the shadowed land around her gradually brightening.

Her first clear glimpse of the castle caused her breath to stick in her throat. Madrigar crowned a broad hill across the valley she overlooked, the numerous windows on its upper levels beginning to flash gold. Arnwall's seat was a hovel compared to this. The structure was almost too big for her to take in. No less than eight stone towers protected the stone fortress, all bristling with ramparts. The bailey alone enclosed more than an acre, its walls sheltering many strong buildings. Grass rolled like a lush green carpet up to the moat.

Violet was pretty sure the ambling flocks of sheep who cropped it were more populous than her whole kingdom.

"Good Lord," she muttered under her breath. How was she going to talk her way in there?

But there was nothing for it except to try. Surely the fairy wouldn't have sent her here if her quest were impossible. Resigned, she dug the snarl of thread from the bundle the fairy had given her. Once she'd retied the rest, she tucked the thread between her breasts next to Etta's small charm bag.

As she did, the clothes she wore tingled on her skin. Startled, she watched the stained silk grow coarser, thicker, until it was as heavy as a potato sack. A weight flopped against her back, and Violet realized her old gown had grown a hood. Taking this as a suggestion, she pulled it over her hair and face. Her soft hands disappeared beneath drooping sleeves—not that they would have given her away in their present state. To her delight, a worn but sturdy pair of boots blinked into being on the ground before her.

At least her feet would be better off.

The magical clothes seemed to have returned a bit of her strength, enough that she could face walking the final distance between her and her goal. She stood carefully, not wanting to disturb her sleeping companion.

"Goodbye," she whispered to the raven. "Thank you ever so for your help."

Chapter 5

P rince Augustin's stallion, Balthus, had gone mad. Two stable boys had been bitten, and another kicked senseless. Finally, the warhorse had to be shut up in one of the smaller buildings they used to separate ungelded stallions from mares in heat.

Augustin watched Balthus there, trotting angrily back and forth across the room that contained him, snapping his teeth at anyone who approached the rails. Stallions were temperamental, but usually he settled for Augustin. This morning, the prince's attempts at soothing were rebuffed along with the rest.

"Did someone tease him?" he asked Geoffrey the stable master. "You know he doesn't like that."

"I'd whip any boy who did," said the older man, a tasseled piece of barley wagging between his lips. He was a head shorter than the prince, and as lean as the whip with which he'd threatened his young charges. "Theory is a pair of Cook's cats chased a mouse through his stall."

"He ought to be calming down."

"Don't know why he's not," the stable master replied.

Two of his boys broke into giggles. The prince looked at them with his eyebrows up.

"The beggar girl can charm him," they spluttered between laughs. "One whiff of her and proud old Balthus will freeze in horror!"

Augustin ignored this second claim to pierce the heart of the matter. "What beggar girl?"

Geoffrey pulled the barley tassel out of his mouth. "Some poor wench who turned up this morning. Claims she's a horse charmer. Plunked herself down beyond the drawbridge and says she won't leave until she's let in." He shrugged. "Probably hoping to cadge a meal."

The hair on Augustin's arms gave an odd prickle. "Did she beg for food?"

"Not that I know of, sire."

"Bring her here," Augustin commanded one of the stable boys.

"Here?" the boy he'd singled out repeated, his jaw hanging.

"Yes, here. None of you has calmed Balthus. Why shouldn't this stranger try?"

He sent the second boy off for bread and cheese. Even if the girl was shamming, she deserved a meal for boldness alone. Geoffrey shook his head at him, probably thinking he'd been gammoned.

The girl who was escorted back was as short as the stable lad, and so slight the prince's ribs contracted to imagine her tramping the roads alone. Thank the saints he'd dispatched those trolls, or she'd never have arrived safely. Aside from her size, her looks were a mystery. From head to toe she was bundled in gray rags.

To be fair to the stable boys, she was a bit odorous.

Augustin doubted Balthus would mind. He was an animal, after all. The girl was a different matter. She eyed his restlessly trotting stallion with unmistakable wariness.

"Well?" Augustin said. "Can you help or not? Don't lie now. I'll feed you no matter what."

The girl pulled herself straighter and turned to him, her air of dignity surprising. A deliciously carnal ripple ran down the length of his cock, lifting it to semi-erectness.

Oh, really, the prince chided his unruly prick. This pushed the boundaries even for him. The girl smelled, and—though he wasn't fussy—she wasn't at all the buxom type he preferred. Given how little he could see of her, she might not even be old enough to decently lust after.

"I can help," she said.

Her words dried the prince's mouth. Oh, she was old enough. The voice that issued from her was soft and husky, as seductive as pussy willows dragged across skin. Had she been hideous—which perhaps she was—those smoky tones would have called to him. He suddenly wanted to hear how she sounded murmuring bed pleas.

He cleared his throat, unwontedly embarrassed. "Do you . . . need assistance with your horse charming?"

"If you would hold him," she said, "I could actually reach his ear."

"We'll wait out here," the stable master said, his mouth suspiciously near a grin. "Balthus likes you best anyway."

Hell, Augustin thought, eyeing his stallion's skittering steps. He turned to pin the beggar girl with his gaze. "Stay well behind until I've got him."

Getting him wasn't easy. In the cursing, snorting battle that ensued, Balthus gifted him with a few bruises. At last, Augustin had the warhorse's neck wrenched down in a wrestler's grip. Balthus was still pretty far off the ground. The beggar girl put her hand on the prince's shoulder so she could lean up. The warmth of her little fingers was a sensation a man like him couldn't fail to note. Less enraptured, Balthus's ear flicked an irate warning.

"Violet loves you," the girl whispered into it.

Whatever powers she called upon, they *were* magic. Balthus released a long horsey sigh, every muscle in his great body relaxing. Cautiously, the prince let go of his neck. The horse's ears and tail settled. His nose bumped Augustin's chest in the friendliest possible manner, as if to ask what all the fuss was about.

"Good Lord," breathed the prince, stupefied.

The beggar girl dropped her hand, leaving his shoulder cold. Balthus nuzzled her for good measure, lipping the sheaf of astonishingly red hair that had slipped from beneath her hood.

"Stop that," Augustin said, swatting the stupid beast even as he noticed how very beautiful the lock was.

The girl stepped back as soon as her hair was free.

Augustin looked at her. She'd drawn her hood back around her face, hiding herself from him. Too bad for her he was a connoisseur of women. He had no trouble spying pretty hands underneath that dirt, or the pretty tip of a nose.

"So," he said, after which he unexpectedly had to swallow. "Shall I—" *kiss you?* supplied the baser side of his nature. "Why don't I find you a place to—" *lie back and spread your legs* "- wash up and, er, break your fast and rest?"

"She could take the sleeping bench in the loft," one of the stable boys volunteered, his mockery changed to awe. "Since Balthus likes her so much."

There was hay in this small barn's loft. And blankets. And plenty of privacy. The prince's prick hardened at the thought of helping her wash up.

"I'd be grateful for a place to stay," the beggar girl admitted.

Was her gorgeous voice a trifle huskier than before, or did the prince simply wish it were?

"Is Violet your name?" he blurted.

She nodded, and for no good reason his pulse quickened. Violet was a beautiful name. Surely the girl who held it was not ugly. His face felt hot, his scalp prickling with sweat. Within the shadow of her rags, her eyes lifted and locked on his. What color they were didn't matter. The air in his lungs thickened.

"I'm Augustin."

One of the stable boys said something he didn't catch.

"Come on, lads," said the stable master. "The prince can take care of this from here."

*

Madrigar's prince had mesmerizing deep blue eyes. For that matter, he had mesmerizing shoulders and arms and thighs, muscles packed onto them so perfectly one inch more would have been too much. Violet didn't think she'd ever seen a man so purely beautiful: from his guinea gold hair, to the health-flushed skin that poured over his chiseled cheekbones, to the way his calves filled his tan breeches. He smelled amazing, which didn't seem fair to her, a mix of meadow and man and leather that flew up her nose like a love philter.

Considering how little her body needed love philters, that was unfair as well.

"This way," he said hoarsely, pointing to the loft ladder.

She went up first with him close behind her. He seemed not to be breathing right, as if he were trying to hide how quickly his lungs wanted to go in and out. Violet's pussy began to melt. She was hardly breathing right herself.

She stumbled slightly as she stepped off the final rung.

"Careful," he said.

By the time he was up himself, she was steady on her feet. He took her elbow the same as if she were teetering. Violet didn't object. Even through her cloak, his touch shot tingles all the way up her arm.

The scent of hay swirled into the scent of him.

"Your sleeping bench is there," he said, his gaze apparently unable to leave hers. "And a little shelf to set out your things. I believe there's water in that basin, but it might not be fresh."

"Thank you." Her voice was thick with arousal. Prince Augustin's beautiful eyes went dark.

"I'm sorry," he said, rather hoarse himself. "I left your packet of food back down in the barn."

Rather than leave, he continued to stare at her, his breath coming faster as it escaped his ability to control it. Violet's cheeks grew hotter, and also other parts of her. The prince's body seemed to struggle before he turned away, as if invisible iron chains had been holding him where he was.

"I'll get it for you," he said, stepping toward the loft ladder.

"Don't."

Her arm flew up of its own volition, the tips of her fingers brushing his bare forearm. The prince froze in place. He wore a snug hunting shirt with the sleeves pushed up. The gilded hair on his arms was silky, the strong tendons underneath warmer than she expected.

Stay, she thought. *Be with me.*

The prince had lowered his head. He turned it back to her, the gaze he slanted from his hooded eyes so hot it made her shudder. "Don't play with fire, Violet."

His warning rumbled from his chest. Violet couldn't speak. She wet her lips, part nervousness, part intense attraction to this beautiful stranger. Augustin spotted the small gesture. His muscles tightened as his face flushed darker.

"God in heaven," he said.

His hands seized her head, one to either side of her ragged hood, pressing it to her ears. As tall as he was, he looked down a height to her. With her head tilted in his palms, she supposed he could see her face.

"You *are* beautiful," he murmured.

She wasn't more than pretty, but when he said it, she believed. Feeling awestruck, she gazed back at him. His golden brows enchanted her, the tiniest furrow marking where they drew together. Even more fascinating were the eyes they shadowed. She didn't understand how they could look simultaneously peaceful and pained.

Something in *her* eyes must have affected him. The little crease deepened on his forehead.

"Violet," he said. "I'm not an ordinary man. There are things about me that could hurt you."

She didn't care. She stretched up on her toes and pulled his head down to hers.

He was groaning by the time their lips met. His mouth brushed hers, his hands on her upper arms, gripping the muscles hard. "Open," he said, nudging her with those beautifully sculpted lips.

"Violet, kiss me."

She shivered and let his tongue slide into her mouth.

The kiss shook her like an earthquake without being the least violent. Slowly, delectably, Augustin penetrated her with his tongue. The surface of his lips was soft, the muscles that moved them firm. She was tempted to run her tongue across them, but that would have interfered with what he was doing. She couldn't help but feel he was claiming her, thrusting that wet silken spear slowly in and out, savoring, teasing, as if his tongue were a much different part of him.

This would have been enough to charm her, but he had other sweets to offer. With a blissful rumble of enjoyment, he changed angles, luring her tongue into his mouth with a spate of delicious suckling that simply could not be resisted. Violet hadn't expected a man so handsome to have such skill. That he could have been more forceful was obvious. Without the slightest effort, he lifted her off her feet to spare his neck the crick it had to be getting. Held safely in his arms, Violet wrapped her legs around him, her eternally aching pussy loving the hardness of his flat muscles.

When she rolled against them, he grunted into her mouth.

It must have been a grunt of approval, because a heartbeat later one big hand was covering her bottom and her back was squashed to the hayloft wall. He wriggled her down so that his big erection rubbed the *v* of her thighs.

Even then he was careful not to hurt her.

"You're so little," he breathed. "I cannot wait to get inside you."

She couldn't wait either. She kissed him harder as he turned them, lowering her back on a pile of blankets laid over wooden planks. Still kissing her, the prince's hand tugged her skirts higher up her legs. He caressed her ankle, her calf, and the lean muscle of her thigh. Violet gasped as his hand slid inside the gap of her linen drawers. He'd closed his fingers around her pussy, palm squeezing her wetness, thumb curving directly over her distended clitoris.

"Christ Almighty," he swore, tearing his mouth free of hers.

She blinked at him, then blushed furiously. She knew what he was feeling.

"You're swollen," he said. "You're a fucking strawberry drenched in cream."

She twisted to get away, but his hand tightened on her flesh, the sudden massage he gave her trapping her where she was, a prisoner to the lust she could never slake. If he did what he was doing a little harder, she was going to come.

"I'm sorry," she burst out, then bit her lip against groaning. "I can't help the way I'm reacting."

If anything, the prince's hand squeezed her harder. "Violet," he growled. "This is the fucking most gorgeous pussy I've ever had the privilege of touching."

He kissed her before she could respond, his tongue plunging deep. Then he wrenched his lips off again. The grin he flashed as he retreated was the wickedest she had ever seen. "You *know* I have to taste you."

Flinging up her skirts, he dragged down her drawers in almost the same motion. She was leaning back on her elbows, her lower legs dangling off the blanketed sleeping bench. Augustin pushed her knees wider and drew in an appreciative breath. The flaring of his nostrils reminded her just how sweaty and mussed she was.

"No," she gasped.

Augustin's dangerous grin broadened, somehow all the more seductive coming from his crouched position between her thighs. His thumbs ran up and down her drenched labia, pulling them wider with the motion. That simple indirect stimulation was sufficient to drag a mortifying whimper from her.

"Yes," Augustin countermanded, then sealed his mouth atop her desperately throbbing pearl.

*

If Augustin could have fallen in love, he'd have fallen for this girl's pussy. Her clit was so engorged with blood it was hot. It rolled like satin against his tongue, as tart as a ripe berry. He suckled it, then tongued it, then rumbled out sounds of rut he could not hold in. When her little hands shoved his shoulders, he barely registered the pressure. The scent of her arousal soaked his brain, the thought that his rigid prick was going to plunge into this treasure.

"Please," she said. "Please, I need to wash up."

"Shush," he soothed, backing off far enough to speak. "You don't smell any worse than my horse."

Her sudden silence warned him he'd committed another of his infamous faux pas. "Thank you very much!" she huffed once she'd recovered.

Her eyes were laughing, so he pressed a light kiss to her berry.

"Oh," she said breathlessly.

He grinned and tickled her most sensitive spot with his fluttering tongue.

"*Oh*," she said, much lower.

On confident ground again, he sank his mouth onto her. Her *ohs* turned to sighs and then into ragged moans. He had to plant his forearms on her hips, because she was soon thrashing desperately. When she came for the first time, the small of her back arched a full two hand spans off the blankets.

"*Anhh*," she cried, the wail of a forest cat.

This delighted him so much he had to make her do it again.

Her hands fumbled to his head, fingers tangling awkwardly in his hair. She seemed like she wanted to urge him closer, but perhaps was embarrassed to. More than happy to help out, he worked his thumbs in firmer circles around what his mouth was doing.

"Oh God," she gasped, hips bucking up at him. "Please keep doing *that*."

He laughed even as she came, as happy as a drunkard in a wine cellar. Women were always swooning underneath him. This girl was made of sterner and apparently lusty stuff. It seemed too much to hope for, but her desire for pleasure might, just maybe, run neck and neck with his.

Grunting at that awe-inspiring thought, he shoved both forearms under her bottom to tip her pelvis to a more advantageous slant. That he could tell she liked. Her arms flew out to grip the edge of the sleeping bench.

"*Augustin*," she groaned.

Augustin didn't think he'd ever been this excited, like a stallion scenting his ideal mare. His prick thrust out from his loins like an iron truss, tenting the front of his clothing. His balls were sucked so tight against his root they ached, and his blood sang hot in his veins. He hurt with his longing to touch his cock, but he couldn't bring himself to take his hands off the girl. He had her at the perfect angle. She was quivering in his arms. For once, his release could wait. He'd pour it into her as soon as she finished. Swamp her with it. Overflow her tight little quim with seething jets by the score.

All right, he'd have to pull out the same as always, but for this moment he could dream.

The blanket tore when she came this time. She'd fisted her hands into it and strained too hard as the spasm hit. Her wail was music to him. When she finally settled, still not swooning, he thought he'd never been so pleased with his skills.

Of course, there were other ways he needed pleasing—rather urgently, to be frank. He only hoped he'd have the strength to withdraw from her. The longing to spill within her was so immense, so instinctive that his ballocks were tied in knots.

He waited until her eyes opened dazedly. They were green, he noticed, like the Southern Sea sparkling in daylight. The fans of her lashes were a slightly darker red than her hair, the same red as the pretty triangle of curls his mouth had been buried in. A very gratified masculine growl rolled around his chest.

She tried to sit up, but he shook his head and smiled for her to stay as she was. Drawing his forearms from underneath her, he sat back on his heels. His hands did not falter on the front of his breeches, practiced fingers swiftly undoing the front ties. He shoved his braies down, pausing to let her gasp at the sight of his turgid prick. Probably she hadn't seen one so large before. Augustin was gifted in that area. He shifted his upper body back over her on his arms. Despite the weightiness of his erection, its stiffness prevented it from hanging more than a finger's distance from his belly.

He felt like its head was sniffing how good she smelled.

"Now," he said, his voice gone dark with anticipation. "Shall we move on to the next course? I hope so. I think I actually might die if I don't get my prick in your sweet pussy."

"Oh!" she cried—and not the kind of *oh* he wanted. "Augustin, I'm sorry, but I mustn't."

"*Mustn't?*"

"I'm sorry. I . . . I promised my father I'd remain a maid until I marry."

He probably shouldn't have cursed the way he did in front of a girl this young, even less so if she was a virgin.

"I'd pull out before I spilled," he said, struggling not to sound angry—or pleading, for that matter. Princes didn't beg for pleasures. "I wouldn't get you with child."

Her hands were pressed to her kiss-bruised mouth, her cheeks stained bright rose. "I'm sorry. I cannot break my vow. I know I shouldn't have let you please me. In my defense, you made me forget myself!"

Not enough, he thought sourly. He was disconcerted—not only by her refusal but also by how much it bothered him. Perhaps she hadn't swooned because he didn't please her as he did his usual partners. Perhaps, being a foreigner, she was more particular than they were. He did up his clothing, trying his best to pretend the throb of his "untiring" sword caused him no discomfort. His prick didn't realize the dalliance was over. It still held out hope for reward. Augustin could have suggested she repay the favor he'd done for her, but Violet had stung his pride. She also wasn't proposing the idea herself. Not that he couldn't find other volunteers to suck him off. Scads of them, before he'd walked a mile.

To his irritation, he found he didn't like that idea. Violet's soft swollen mouth was the one he wanted. She was the wench who owed him.

The prince's frown was as mighty as his arousal. He pushed to his feet stiffly.

"Do forgive me," he said coolly. "We can only hope your future husband pleases you better than I have."

Chapter 6

I f Violet hadn't been so exhausted—*and pleasured*, her conscience reminded—she wouldn't have slept a wink. Her bed certainly wasn't the soft mattress she was used to. She did sleep, however, and soundly. Only when she woke in the loft the next morning did her worries press in on her.

The first sight that met her eyes was the fairy's walnut, sitting pretty as you please on the blanket beside her head.

Violet knew she hadn't removed the charm from its tied bundle. Her stomach clenched as the fairy's instructions for how to use it rushed back to her. Given how angry Prince Augustin had been after she refused him, following those instructions seemed ill advised.

A single speck of fairy dust twinkled on the nut in the morning sun, as good as nagging her to keep her promise.

"Fine," she said, flinging off the sleeping bench to wash up. She knew her fairy tales same as any girl. Obedience to those wiser than one's self was always rewarded.

One of the stable boys must have brought her fresh water. Clean rags sat beside the basin, folded in a neat stack. With a quick glance around to ensure she could not be watched, Violet pulled off her enchanted rags and put the water to its much-needed use.

The sponge bath would have been quicker if her arousal hadn't woken along with her. Violet saw to it because Bojik's curse left her little choice. If she didn't work herself to a few releases, she wouldn't be able to concentrate. She didn't mean to think of the prince as she sought her temporary cure, but memories rose anyway. The image of his quick hands opening his clothing, of his thick red cock thrusting free, made her releases harder and more delicious than usual.

*

Prince Augustin hadn't planned to spy on the beggar girl. Unable to sleep, he'd tossed and turned until daybreak. At cock's crow, he realized his guest—however infuriating she might be—needed to be

29

supplied with basic amenities.

It was hardly his job to supply them, nor was it appropriate for him to creep in while she was sleeping to set them out. Most certainly, he should not have performed the task without first seeing to his ferocious morning erection. He had, though, avoiding the breakfast maid and her tray with an adeptness that seemed sheer foolishness now.

On the other hand, how was he to know the beggar girl would have the body of a pocket goddess without her clothes?

Crouched behind a stack of bales, the prince struggled not to moan at the sight of her. Violet's breasts were rounded and high—not large but fuller than he'd expected. Nipples the size of cherries pouted temptingly at their tips, begging to be sucked and pinched by a man like him. Her skin was velvet, pale as cream where it wasn't flushed. It poured down her compact curves, swooped in at her little waist, then flared out for her hips and her tight bottom. Augustin had to swallow at the strength of her legs, which could have been designed for wrapping around a man. Though her hair was disheveled, her rich red braid hung thick as rope to her ankles.

Picturing that braid undone slammed his arousal higher with the force of a battering ram.

His cock stretched to such proportions he thought it might burst his skin. The head breached the gap of his underclothes, the blood that throbbed within it nudging it against his breeches. Though he longed to stroke it, he feared the noises he was bound to make would lead to discovery. That was a humiliation he could do without. He fisted his hands instead, nails pricking sharply into his palms.

When she began pleasuring herself, digging the dampened washcloth between her labia, the pain that stabbed through his erection was like nothing he'd known before.

She was quick about the business, as if this were a common task for her to perform. She braced one hand on the crate where the washbasin sat and shoved the other between her legs. Her little feet were firmly planted, the muscles in her curvy legs cording. She made a sound as she came, soft and guttural. Augustin's cock found this so inspiring, a small spurt of sexual emissions hit the inside of his trousers. He gasped, but Violet didn't hear.

She was too busy rubbing herself to release again.

Six times she did this, each orgasm appearing as necessary to her as the one before. The succeeding peaks seemed to grow more intense. For her final climax, she flung her head back and groaned, her beautiful body stiff, her upper teeth digging into her lower lip. When she dropped the rag she'd used to frig herself, her gorgeous berry stood out from her folds like the reddened tip of a small finger.

The prince was panting so violently he could only breathe through his mouth. Lust wracked his erection, its slit trickling steadily. Violet dampened the last clean cloth, cleansing the sheen of sweat from her succulent body. She grimaced as she stroked its roughness across her rose pink nipples.

Was it possible she wanted still more pleasure?

The chance that she might had the prince's brain very close to exploding.

If she did want more, she was ignoring it. She wrapped herself in her rags again. The thought that she was clean beneath them tormented him. Perhaps he made a sound. She looked around the loft as if something had spooked her. Frowning, she grabbed an object he hadn't noticed from the sleeping bench. Then she left him to his privacy.

He could scarcely wait for her to finish going down the ladder. As soon as she had, he drove his shaking right hand into his breeches, not bothering to untie them. Making sure the knob was in the open was good enough; he didn't want to leave a worse wet spot. With a muffled grunt, he wrapped his left hand around the leather that cupped his balls. That done, he was ready to go. One upward stroke wrenched a gasp from him. Two told him he'd better fist himself faster. The skin of his shaft burned like it had been set afire, almost too thick to hold. Pressure gathered at the base of his spine, the trickle of precum oiling the work of his hand. Faster he pumped his cockstand, harder, until his hips jerked forward and the strongest orgasm of his life blasted free. The ejaculation wrung his balls dry, the strength of his pleasure unnervingly close to pain.

He was almost sated enough for his prick not to rise again. He assured himself it wasn't due to the girl. He'd skipped his morning bed play, and then he'd had to crouch here watching her get off. Any man would have climaxed hard after that. As if to mock him, his knees wobbled when he pushed to his feet. A great deal of semen had spattered his hand and arm, starting to dry and get sticky.

He looked toward the bowl of water the beggar girl had used.

"No," he said. "You are not going to wash yourself with the same cloth as a woman who turned you down."

He did, though. He couldn't seem to stop himself. For the rest of the day, he could smell both their scents mingled on his body.

*

The prince was *not* going to dwell on the beggar girl's perverseness. He breakfasted with this mother's guests—two of them anyway. The princesses of Llyr were dressed in the newest fashion. Their peach and daffodil velvet gowns fitted snugly to their waists, rather than cinching under their bosoms. Augustin didn't pay much attention to women's clothing unless he was removing it. Nonetheless, he thought they looked pretty and told them so.

Had she been at the table, his mother would have approved.

The elder sister lifted a spoonful of coddled egg. "Is the food not to your liking? You've barely consumed a bite."

Tastes like sawdust, he began to say, then realized this was the sort of thing lovesick knights nattered on about in stories—generally right before they wasted away.

"Delicious," he said, shoving a bite in his mouth. "I was distracted by my beautiful company."

"Thank goodness," the younger sister said archly. "I appreciate a man with an appetite."

Her tinkling laugh annoyed him, though it wouldn't have normally. Of the two sisters, her body was the type he preferred, so round and healthy a man could happily bounce on it for hours.

"We've heard you're a marvelous horseman," the elder said, no lighter with her entendre than her sibling. "Perhaps you'd be kind enough to take us."

"We did don our riding costumes," interjected the younger.

If those were riding costumes, Augustin was a cow. They'd split their seams at the first hint of a canter. He frowned at his fancy porcelain plate, noticing he was forgetting to eat again.

"Eugenie—" he began.

"*Emmanuelle*," the younger said with a fetching pout. This wasn't the first time she'd corrected him. "My sister is Eugenie."

"Right. Princesses . . ."

"Don't refuse us!" the elder cried. "We simply must admire your famous form as you sit astride."

Augustin threw in the towel . . . or at least his napkin. "As you wish. We'll see what mounts we can find for you."

*

Augustin had intended to steer clear of the stables. As he'd feared, the staff had made Violet their new pet. It was she who led out the mares for the princesses. The hour was early and the beasts were fresh, not yet having been exercised. With Violet's hand on their bridles, they walked into the yard as docile as lambs.

"Oh, how quaint," said the sister he thought was Emmanuelle. "Madrigar provides occupation for the less fortunate."

Violet stiffened but handed off the reins with a small curtsey. The younger sister accepted her mare silently. Violet looked a child beside her, too short and small to ever be called handsome. She stroked the mare's mane in parting and turned to him.

She didn't speak, simply stared at him with her big green eyes. Her rags weren't pulled as closely around her face as before. He saw she'd rubbed dirt onto her cheeks, though this couldn't hide her beauty. His throat felt unusually tight. Why did this humble girl refuse him? Pet or not, she was a stranger. No one would have told her he had no heart . . . unless she simply sensed the wrongness in him?

To hell with her, he thought, lifting his chin proudly. "Bring Balthus," he ordered.

She curtseyed more deeply to him than she had to Emmanuelle. After she left, Augustin waited, and waited, and finally hissed in a breath of outrage at the beast she led out.

Somehow, the beggar girl had found a donkey that resembled his prize warhorse. The creature had the same deep black coat, the same white sock on his right hind foot. The stable yard exploded with laughter as grooms and boys turned to see what was going on. To add to her offense, Violet had dressed the donkey in Balthus's saddle. Hell, she'd braided a chain of daisies into the creature's tail!

Choking noises came from the two princesses. If *they* were laughing, Augustin didn't want to know.

"What is the meaning of this?" he asked. "I told you to bring Balthus."

"This *is* Balthus."

Two stable boys fell over clutching their stomachs, they were laughing so hard. Augustin ground his teeth together, hating that his cheeks stung hot with embarrassment. "Bring me Balthus," he repeated.

Violet sighed as if she regretted what she was doing. With half her attention, she petted the black fur on the donkey's nose. "I swear to you, on my honor, this is your horse Balthus." She bit her lip and swallowed. Augustin tensed at whatever she was girding herself to say. Her right hand clenched in a little fist.

"*The true prince sees beyond appearances,*" she burst out.

Her voice rang across the yard. To judge by her flush, she hadn't meant to speak that loudly. Shocked at last by the stranger's boldness, the merriment around them died.

"Care to repeat that?" Augustin asked softly.

She leaned closer, speaking only to him. "The true prince sees beyond appearances. Please, your highness. Mount him and you will see."

Both Augustin's eyebrows rose. "*Mount* him?"

"Your people love you, your highness. They will not think less of you if you go along with their fun."

He gaped at her, staggered by her cheek. A beggar girl, giving *him* advice about his people.

"Please," she said humbly. Beside her, as if it were agreeing, the donkey jerked its head up and down.

He had no reason to trust her, and couldn't say precisely why he gave in. The plea in her eyes perhaps, or his knowledge that his sense of humor regarding himself wasn't always the best.

"Very well," he said. "I will ride 'Balthus.'"

Cheers broke out around the bailey, taking some of the sting from the earlier laughter. Resigned to get through this, the prince swung into the saddle, the donkey short enough to make this no chore. Unfortunately, in addition to being short, the donkey had a belly like a rain barrel. Augustin's legs stuck out as he made a circuit around the yard. He did his best to play along with the cheering, nodding gravely and waving at his admiring audience.

By the third turn around the dirt, he'd had quite enough. Servants from other parts of the castle were starting to stick their heads out the windows that overlooked the courtyard. Augustin rocked back in the saddle in preparation for dismounting. As he did, something snapped underneath his rear. He reached around to remove whatever it was and found a large walnut, split neatly down the middle. Inside, where a nut should have been, was a white sugar cube. Augustin tipped it into his palm and stared, hardly noticing that the donkey had stopped walking.

When he looked up, Violet was grinning at him from the front of the crowd. She looked so happy, so *approving* that for a moment he lost his breath. It occurred to him that sugar cubes were Balthus's favorite treat in the world.

Ah, he thought. *More magic.*

He swung out of the saddle, holding up the white cube for all to see. Then, with a flourish he hadn't known he had in him, he fed the confection to the donkey.

If he hadn't seen it with his own eyes, he wouldn't have believed. The air around the fat donkey shimmered, and sparkled, and suddenly his stallion Balthus stood before him, noisily chomping his reward. Balthus wore his own tack and saddle. The only change from his usual was the daisies wound through his contentedly swishing tail.

The corners of the prince's mouth tugged up. He couldn't deny the lethal warhorse looked cute.

"Very clever," he conceded to Violet, his compliment covered up by the general *oohs* and *ahs.*

"Extraordinary!" Eugenie or maybe Emmanuelle exclaimed behind him. "Madrigar is indeed a kingdom of wonders!"

Augustin could not respond. He was too busy watching Violet clap for him, seeming more pleased on his behalf than she was at pulling off this marvel. A knot of warmth swelled within his breast. The tangle hurt, but it felt good as well.

Almost as if he did have a heart in there.

Chapter 7

A ugustin arrived for the evening meal "dressed like a proper prince," as his mother was wont to say. Snug black hose encased his legs, with a short, pleated sky-blue tunic to top them off. His full sleeves were slashed, and his black velvet cap bore a small feather. He'd brushed his shoulder-length wavy hair and shaved. All in all, he looked the part the queen wanted him to play.

He was afraid looks were as deep as it went. As little attention as he was paying, the musicians up on the balcony might as well have been squawking birds.

He kept seeing Violet beaming at him across the stable yard.

Women didn't smile at him that way. They seduced. They flirted. In Eugenie's case, they simpered. Sometimes they giggled like girls when he bedded them. They didn't smile as if they were happy *for* him, as if he might be worth admiring for more than his masculine beauty or his sexual prowess.

Violet smiled at him like a friend would do.

He shook his head at the servant who was offering him a meat platter. His plate was full of things he was not eating. He sipped his wine, then twirled his silver soupspoon around his fingers. Because he wasn't being careful, he failed to evade his mother's meaningful frown. She probably wanted him to converse with the princesses. His father sat at the table's head beside her, smiling faintly at everyone. The king of Madrigar was so genial, so sweet natured and biddable that it was no wonder his mother ran the country.

What Augustin needed was a wife whose nature was more like Violet's. With a queen like her, they could rule side by side.

The thought shocked his fingers into fumbling on his spoon. The utensil spun through the air and fell with a loud clatter.

"Bad luck!" Eugenie declared with her tinkling laugh.

"No, it's good luck," Emmanuelle contradicted. "It means company is coming."

If *they* were the company, Augustin thought they both had the right of it. Patience snapping like a twig, he rose from his chair and bowed.

"Forgive me," he said when everyone looked at him. "I have personal business I must see to."

He saw the glare his mother shot him but stubbornly ignored it. His steps lengthened to strides as he left the room, eagerness speeding through his veins. He had the irrepressible sensation that freedom was just one leap ahead—though he knew that was unlikely.

Pride be damned. He couldn't hold the bowstring a moment longer. He had to take another shot at his beggar girl.

*

Violet didn't know whose decision it had been to leave Balthus in the spacious stall underneath her loft. Maybe the horse had determined it. He looked suspiciously pleased with himself as she brushed the currycomb down his side.

Squares of moonlight slanted in the barn windows, allowing her to work without a lantern. Violet often cared for her mare this way. To her, the steady stroke of the brush was soothing. As she found a spot Balthus liked having rubbed on his croup, he blew out his breath and stood hipshot. He was a huge animal, far taller than she was and all rippling muscle under his gleaming coat. She should have been intimidated, but when he swung his head around and smugly batted his equine lashes, she couldn't be anything but amused.

To her relief, he seemed none the worse for having been temporarily turned into a donkey.

"I know your secret," she murmured. "Let a woman get her hands on you, and you're nothing but a big baby."

"Some would say all males are."

Every nerve in her body tingled.

"Augustin," she said, remembering too late she should call him *your highness*.

He certainly looked nice enough to deserve the formal address. He leaned in the moonlit entrance with his strong arms crossed and his church-door shoulders casting a broad shadow. The princesses' lovely gowns had given her a sting this morning, but they paled next to his outfit. The prince's tunic and hose were finer than anything she owned, and so well fitted she had no trouble picturing how he'd look naked. He must have been accustomed to them. He didn't seem worried about dirtying them here.

37

He pushed off from his perch as she stared, the way he stalked toward her making her nervous and very wet. His legs were gorgeous in those tight hose. She couldn't help wishing she could see his rear view too.

Remember the fairy's warning. If you let this man inside your body, you'll forget everything you owe your people.

Her tempter stopped outside the metal gate to the stall, a barrier Violet doubted was stout enough. She struggled to speak lightly. "Does this visit mean you've forgiven me for embarrassing you?"

His mouth slanted on one side, its lush shape apparent even in the low light. "I could be convinced to."

His voice was husky. Violet's tongue crept out to her lips.

"Come out of there," he coaxed. "Thanks to you spoiling him, Balthus has fallen asleep."

She came, but only because she didn't want to disturb the horse. Well, not *only* because of that. The prospect of being close to Augustin also drew her. He took her hands, tugging the tips of her sturdy boots to his jeweled slippers. A tremor that had as much to do with nerves as desire skittered across her shoulders.

Though she was a princess herself, he seemed far too grand for her.

"What do you want of me?" she asked, gazing the long distance up to him.

His long-fingered hand smoothed a fallen lock behind her ear. "Everything," he said, watching his movements and not her eyes, "but I would settle for you balancing the scales between us."

She didn't need his heated gaze to explain what he meant. Her nipples swelled and tightened, her clit tickling the folds that protected it. Those three sharp points pulsed in time to her quickening heartbeat. "You want me to take your prick in my mouth."

Again the prince stroked the side of her face, finishing with one thumb pressed to the dent in her lower lip. "I'd love to feel this pretty mouth on me. If you're shy, I can teach you what I like."

Violet's grin broke out before she could stop it. He might be surprised to know how little *teaching* she required. "I promised my father I would remain a maid, not that I was innocent."

*

Augustin had seen expressions like hers before. Their feyness almost always led to heady pleasures. His body should have reacted as usual: with healthy but not dramatic interest. Instead, his pulse careened straight into a gallop, his already eager cock punching a good inch longer in his codpiece.

Still smiling, Violet put her hands on his waist. Her fingers were hot, her thumbs gently squeezing his taut muscles. That small compression made his cock lurch toward her again. The reaction must have been strong enough to see.

Violet quirked her brows at him. "Are you sure you're ready for this?"

"I am," he rasped, too aroused to be embarrassed.

She began nudging him backward. "You'd better lean your shoulders against that wall."

She was suggesting his legs wouldn't hold him up. That didn't seem possible; he was extremely fit and no stranger to this act. All the same, he let her direct him. When he was positioned as she thought good, her hands slid down the sides of his hips and legs. The shiver this stirred surprised him. Maybe she *was* going to have more than the usual effect.

She was on her knees, reaching under his hip-length tunic for the points that held up his hose. Augustin abruptly found himself unable to leave everything to her.

"I want to remove this," he said, wrenching out of his constricting tunic. He tossed it somewhere, his eyes closing heavily as her hands slid under his linen shirt to his bare torso.

How good her touch felt shocked him. Had his nerves been asleep before meeting her? He'd never thought that to be the case, but his breath came faster as her fingertips skimmed his belly's ridges. Light as air, they whispered around his navel, tickling the curly edge of his pubic hair. It was a tease he wasn't sure he could stand. The veins in his cock beat like soldiers marching, the tip leaking heat for her. If she didn't touch it, he was going to die.

She undid the fastenings of his codpiece and let it fall.

"Please," he said, then clamped his jaw against more begging.

She ran the back of her slender fingers up the thick under ridge, her head close enough to his groin that her breath fanned him. At the top of her stroke, she turned her hand so she could drag her fingertips down the reverse route. The delicacy of the caress made his balls shiver.

"You're beautiful everywhere," she marveled.

She pulled her second hand up his thigh, ruffling the hair along it before curving her palm gently around his testicles. He groaned deep in his chest, unable to keep it in.

"Move your feet apart," she said.

For some unholy reason, being told to do so by her caused his prick to jerk higher. The hand that cupped his balls pushed farther around them. Her fingertips found the stretch of smoothness between his anus and scrotum, pressing firmly and kneading it. The prince's teeth nearly split his lip. Sensation spread out from her palpations in hot tight waves. His sphincter clenched on itself. It felt like Violet was squeezing pleasure straight into his prostate.

"Jesus," he gasped. "All right, you've done this before."

She laughed, the chuckle so smugly pleased he couldn't help smiling. She'd known all along what she was doing. "Shall I suck you now, your highness?"

He answered by spearing his fingers into the night-cooled silk of her hair. His eyes had been closed before, but this he had to watch.

She bowed to him like a dream, lips parted, breath coming quick and warm. When her lips molded to his crest, another shock kicked through him. Her mouth was soft and just wet enough. She pushed an impressive ways down his shaft, not quickly but with her tongue rubbing sweet delight into his underside. Those licking motions felt a bit too good for his self control.

As to that, watching his cock slide into her mouth pushed him too close to the edge. Panting, he pulled one hand from her hair and curled it into a fist, hoping this would help him restrain his urge to shove straight into her throat. Experienced or not, she wouldn't welcome that. Continuing to torment him, she pulled up as slowly as she'd gone down, her rosy lips a band of tight satin around his shaft. Then only the head of his prick was in her.

The sound he made must have warned her he was losing control. Clever girl that she was, she wrapped her right hand around his base, pushing it toward his groin. Her hold was snug enough to stretch his skin even tauter along his length. The trick pushed his nerves closer to the surface. When her tongue lapped his glans, her taste buds rasped it deliciously.

A curse tore from him. She did it again and suckled at the same time. The side of his fist thumped the wall behind him.

"Don't stop," he said before she could ask him if all was well. "I'm just . . . not used to waiting."

Her lips curved as she sank on him. From what he'd seen, she wasn't used to waiting either—which didn't mean she was going to rush. She wound him up in tormenting stages, pulling him ever closer to destruction, until he simply had to bury his second hand in her hair again. She'd combed her locks at some point, and the strands were pure silk.

He wanted to whimper, or perhaps just to weep. Pride alone kept him from succumbing.

"Keep your hand on my root," he warned, his throat so tight with strain it was hard to speak. "I need to thrust now. I don't think I can stop myself."

To his amazement, though she didn't release her grip, she pushed it closer to his torso, allowing her mouth access to more of him. He drove forward with a sound that wasn't strictly manly. Humming with approval, Violet sucked him as he went in.

The hot suction could have tumbled fortresses to the ground; it was that pleasurable. Her tongue was genius, her palate a marvelous sleek hardness to push his cock across. He groaned as her cheeks pulled on him, and gasped when her tongue fluttered. They both began to move faster, her swallowed cries an oddly close complement to his. The wetness of her mouth created a clicking sound. When Augustin's cods drew higher, her cupping hand followed them.

"*Violet*," he growled, his hips snapping forward for his next thrust. He was going to come. He could feel the giant wave building at the base of his spine. "Violet, if you . . . don't want me pouring down your throat, you had . . . better let go now."

She wasn't going to. The heel of her palm pressed firmly over his balls. The extra pressure excited him behind bearing. He snarled, and thrust, and Violet's cheeks hollowed.

He needed the wall, after all, if only to brace and push. Knees locked, he came in a flood of heat, as hard as he had this morning, pouring his ecstasy down her throat just as he'd warned her. Selfish though it was, coming in her mouth was almost as good as coming in her pussy. He was surrounded, sucked on and wrapped in warmth. The orgasm peaked incredibly, then let go. Peace washed through him, the claws of his hands relaxing in her hair.

She released him sooner than he wanted, but when she pressed a kiss to his hip and let her cheek rest there, he forgot to mind.

*

Violet loved the feel of his graceful fingers combing through her hair. She was aroused, of course, but curiously content. The groan Augustin had rumbled out when he climaxed still echoed in her ears.

The taste of him in her mouth was amazingly intimate.

"I think I need to sit," he said, laughing shakily.

She smiled as he slid down the wall. When he was settled, he pulled her into his lap. His arms wrapped warmly around her, one hand nudging her head onto his shoulder. Since this was where she wanted it anyway, Violet didn't resist.

"There," he said. "That's better than fighting."

Had they been fighting? If they had, Violet didn't want to dwell on it. She dragged her face up his neck, enjoying the salty smell of his skin where his shirt left off.

"Don't start me up again," he said drowsily. "I'm enjoying being replete for once."

He didn't seem to want her to move otherwise, so Violet relaxed. She knew a bit of men, obviously, but couldn't remember snuggling so peacefully into one before. With a grunt of pleasure, he stirred a bit under her.

"Violet," he said, "why are you traveling alone? What happened to your family?"

The fairy had warned her he had a horror of noble females, so Violet answered cautiously. "My parents were stolen by the seal people."

"Stolen?"

"We think they may have been taken to that race's kingdom under the sea. The local fisherman couldn't track them. Wherever they're being held—" *if* they were being held "- it's too far away for rescue."

"But why? What use could the were-seals have for a few peasants?"

Because he probably didn't mean to insult her parents, Violet shoved off a pinch of anger. "I couldn't say, your highness."

The prince rubbed his jaw against the top of her head. "I like when you call me Augustin. And I am sorry for your loss."

He sounded sincere—and a bit surprised by himself. Perhaps he was surprised. To him, her position could not have been humbler.

Violet wondered if she'd have expressed an equal sorrow for someone lesser born. She hoped so. A future queen ought not to think her pain more important than everyone else's.

Seeing how he did this so easily, she asked herself if the fairy might not have underestimated his decency. Augustin might not need to be tricked into helping her. If she could gain his aid honestly, Violet knew she'd rather.

"What is it?" he asked as she tilted her face to him. "What do you wish of me?"

Violet told him everything.

*

Prince Augustin had been girding himself to accept an unwelcome truth. The orgasm he'd had that morning after watching Violet frig herself had not been a fluke. Tonight's was just as potent, even taking into account her skill with her mouth.

He told himself he wasn't jealous of the men who'd experienced that skill before him. Jealousy required one to have a capacity to care. Nor was he going to allow himself to become obsessed with plunging into her hot pussy. Every woman had the right to preserve her virtue. It shouldn't matter to him that the maidenhead in question belonged to a beggar girl. So what if his mind spun with ways to convince her to give it up? He had no reason to be unsettled by his response to her.

Her answer to his question was as good as dashing ice water on his prick.

Then again, maybe it was the empty cavity in his chest that had frozen over. Everything she'd done since arriving in Madrigar had been calculated to lead him here. Her friendly smiles. Her feats of magic. The soul-shaking bliss that even now reverberated through his body. Maybe she'd been aware of him watching her in that loft. He'd known women to try such ploys.

He'd simply never been seduced for his sword arm before.

He eased her off his lap as gently as he could while simultaneously boiling. He didn't watch her as she came to her feet. He might have felt compelled to offer her his hand. Instead, he tied his hose up with stiff fingers.

Thus braced, he met her deceptively worried eyes. He spoke as coolly as rage allowed. "As much as I admire your loyalty to a kingdom that allowed your parents to be carried off, it is your rulers' place to seek champions."

Violet's breath trailed out on a sigh. "Augustin," she said, her use of his Christian name even then giving him a thrill. "I *am* Arnwall's ruler. My parents were our king and queen. I'm Princess Violet."

For a hanging moment, the prince could not shut his jaw. This got worse and worse. Violet, his succulent beggar girl, was yet another damned princess. So much for his delusion that freedom was a leap away. He wondered if the were-wolf she claimed was preying on her people even existed. The journey to her kingdom likely would provide opportunities for closeness. If Augustin could be cozened into taking her maidenhead, he'd be caught handily.

Far from needing a wife whose nature was more like Violet's, Augustin now prayed the Lord would keep such serpents away from him.

That there was a flaw in his logic he was too furious to examine.

"Did my mother put you up to this?" he demanded.

Violet's mouth formed an annoyingly tempting O. "Your mother! I swear, your highness, I've never met the woman!"

She seemed truthful, but really how could he tell?

"I'm afraid you'll have to forgive me," he said, stooping for his discarded tunic. "I won't be available to hare off on your little quest. I've plenty of dragons to slay close by. Never any shortage, as it happens."

Violet pulled herself straighter, her diminutive dignity irritating him all the more. "That's your answer? You're not willing to help my people?"

He fought the twinge of guilt that flicked through him. "You said yourself your were-wolf has slain no man. My time is too valuable to waste rescuing sheep. What's more, I think you should leave at daybreak tomorrow morn. If you are a princess as you say, you've no need of Madrigar's charity."

Violet's eyes narrowed into slits his mother would have been hard-pressed to outdo. "Believe me," she said, her iciness matching his. "Charity is the last thing I want from you!"

She spun away, her clear attempt to storm off spoiled by the fact she had nothing better than a loft ladder to stump up.

Only when she disappeared at the top did Augustin remember he ought to leave as well.

*

Violet knew she'd let her temper run away with her. She sat on the sleeping bench, swiping off angry tears as she alternated between fuming over Augustin's arrogance and furious shame at herself.

She was Arnwall's ruler. She should have shown more control. A few dozen slaughtered sheep might not impress him, but to her people they could mean the difference between a lean year and one they could not survive. What did Augustin know of hunger, with his fancy slippers and his big castle?

Her hand clenched on an object she didn't remember picking up: the fairy's tied silk bundle with its single remaining charm. Violet scowled at it, reminded anew that she'd brought this bitter disappointment upon herself. She'd been warned not to tell Augustin who she was.

She started to fling the charm away but stopped. Yes, the prince had refused her, but could she afford to accept his answer?

Bojik had killed no man . . . yet. Giving him what he wanted would not guarantee that stayed true. The were-wolf was volatile. Violet had only to displease him once, and he might consider lashing out justified. Indeed, every hour she was absent from her home could be one in which he rampaged among her people.

Violet covered her face, horror at that idea at last drying all her tears.

No matter what her pride preferred, she *had* to follow the guidance the fairy had given her.

Chapter 8

D espite his anger at Violet and himself, the prince had slept a few hours. Being rested cleared his head enough to concede one point. Violet wasn't trying to lure him to her kingdom in hopes of seducing him on the journey. If all she'd wanted were for him to deflower her royal virtue—and thus oblige him to marry her—she'd have done it already. The were-wolf who was thinning her people's flocks probably did exist.

Which didn't mean his other complaints against her were baseless.

He enumerated them as he strode to the stables, grumbling under his breath. Without question, she was deceitful, possibly an evil sorceress, and only interested in what he could do for her in his monster-slaying capacity. She'd led him to believe she liked him for *him*. If he'd had a heart, which she had no reason to know he lacked, this would pile the sin of cruelty atop the rest. She seemed to have no compunction about wasting his time on a trivial threat, though admittedly were-wolves did in many cases move on to human prey.

Augustin pressed a fist to his sternum, the spot behind it aching like he'd swallowed a stone. No woman should have to bed a monster, not peasant and not princess. A temporary reprieve from Bojik's sheep-killing habits wasn't worth the sacrifice. Her other faults aside, Violet was wise to assume the were-wolf's restraint wouldn't last. The way he'd cursed her proved he had no honor. He'd hold her hostage to his beastly standards of right and wrong, her kingdom punished for every imaginary infraction. The pain within the prince's ribcage intensified. What was the matter with Violet's people that *they* wouldn't band together to protect her against this man?

"Sire?" inquired a voice beside his shoulder.

The stable master had joined him in the empty yard. Geoffrey looked half asleep, no surprise considering the sun was just then breaching the horizon. The castle walls cast the yard in shadow, a few dim stars still visible overhead.

"Do you need something?" Geoffrey asked.

46

Tell me the beggar girl hasn't left. Show me any way to earn her forgiveness that doesn't involve saying I was wrong.

He hadn't been wrong . . . or not more than partly.

"Is Balthus awake?" he asked, reluctant to check his stallion's new stall himself.

"Ah," Geoffrey said. He shoved his coif back to scratch his silver hair. "He seems to have eaten something that disagreed with him. That's why I'm up. I don't think he'll be in a shape to be ridden for a few days. Shall I saddle another mount for you?"

Augustin pressed his lips together. "Is Violet with him?"

"No, your highness. The beggar girl appears to have slipped away. Those sorts do, you know. Itchy feet. Rather be out on the open road."

Augustin fought a frown at Geoffrey's obvious sympathy. Did all the servants know he'd taken a shine to the girl?

The princess, he reminded himself. Violet was a princess.

"Saddle any horse that's awake," he said. "I'll ride out through the gatehouse."

"Would you like an escort?"

Augustin shook his head. A man with an untiring sword, whom no weapon forged by man or fae could harm, hardly needed protection.

Geoffrey took the prince at his word about saddling any horse that was up. Destrier was the laziest gelding in the stable—that is, when he wasn't spooking at butterflies and bucking off his riders. Augustin grimaced as the sleepy stable master passed him the reins. The way his head was hanging, Destrier didn't look any more alert than his caretaker.

"Right," Geoffrey said, waving vaguely as he turned away. "Have a safe ride out there."

Augustin suspected the older man was going back to bed. Ah, well. Chances were Violet was long gone. He wasn't going to catch her on any mount, good or bad. He kicked the gelding into action out of mere principle, nodding at the pair of guards who wheeled down the drawbridge for him.

When asked, they claimed the earlier watch must have let Violet out.

The morning was quiet, a cat-gray fog beginning to swirl and settle in the valley. Cook fires were being lit in the castle's town, the bend of their smoke telling him the wind blew out of the east. Augustin rode into its freshness, working Destrier to a trot and then a slow canter. The gelding had smooth paces for a lazy slug and could go quite a distance without stopping. Augustin turned him toward the crook of a nearby stream where a cluster of apple trees hid the bank from view. If Violet had not immediately begun her journey, she might be stopping there. He could offer her the loan of a guard to escort her home. She was a princess. No matter what her offenses, she shouldn't travel alone.

The idea of offering this pleased him. It was coolheaded and considerate. Heartless or not, Augustin could be both those things. Let Princess Violet be the one who ran off in a fit of pride. Augustin was a gentleman.

His mood lightened further when he spotted signs of a camp exactly where he'd expected. He slid off Destrier to cross the stream and examine them, first looping the horse's reins around a low tree branch. Flattened reeds gave evidence of someone sitting, while small bare footsteps in the squishy ground suggested the sitter might indeed have been Violet. A pile of clothes and a pair of boots stashed between two roots confirmed his suspicion. He'd recognize those sorry rags anywhere.

His prick hardened so abruptly his head went light.

If Violet had disrobed, perhaps she was bathing. The last time he'd seen her naked rushed back to him. Evidently, he was interested in doing so again.

A panicked neigh and a clatter of hooves on rocks spun him around in time to see Destrier scrambling frantically up and over the opposite bank. The prince called for him to return, but the stupid beast was too frightened to heed him.

The cheerful flutter of a small white moth told him what had happened.

"Bloody hell," he griped. He should have tied the horse properly. Now he'd have a nice long tramp afoot to the castle—and probably more teasing once he arrived.

He swore more bitterly over that.

It occurred to him that following Violet would put the dubious pleasure off.

He'd almost decided to when a soft whuffling sound turned him back the other way. His breath caught in his throat and stayed there.

A golden horse with a golden saddle had appeared atop the next rise, both horse and tack set ablaze by the young sunlight. Augustin had never seen a mare so lovely, so beautifully conformed and sleek. She was gazing directly at him, her great eyes liquid and soft.

"Well," Augustin murmured, not wanting to spook her. "What are you doing here, sweetheart?"

The mare and her gear were fine enough to belong to a noble lady, even the High Queen herself. Augustin took a cautious step closer, at which the mare backed up.

"Don't be afraid," he soothed. "I just want to lead you back to my stables until we discover who you belong to."

The mare nickered at him and tossed her head.

Taking this as encouragement, Augustin climbed the rest of the slope to her. The mare let him stroke her and check her for injuries. Aside from being a trifle skittish around a stranger, she seemed perfectly healthy.

"Well, then," Augustin said, seized by such a strong urge to try her paces that he knew he wouldn't resist. "Why don't we see how you and I get on?"

She didn't so much as sidle when he tucked his foot into her stirrup and leaped astride. To his delight, his weight didn't trouble her at all.

"You're a strong one, aren't you?"

He took up the reins and turned her, careful not to pull too hard on her undoubtedly sensitive mouth. She responded without objection, as if she'd been his mount since birth.

Then an odd little shiver rippled back through her golden hide.

She took off without warning, like she'd been shot from a catapult. Augustin had to fling his upper body forward or he'd have been thrown off.

"Hey," he crooned, patting her side to calm her. Despite his surprise, he laughed in exhilaration at her impressive burst of speed. "Where do you think you're going?"

Rather than settle, the mare rolled her eyes back and galloped faster. Now Augustin wasn't just holding on, he was holding on for dear life. He tried to turn the mare toward the castle, but this didn't seem to be where she wished to go. Her thundering hooves were untiring, her golden mane whipping back at him. Much too soon for comfort, trees rose in a dark line before them, taller and more ominous than a fortress wall.

The mare was heading straight for the Wailing Wood.

Hell, Augustin thought—and then, *Hell, no.*

This was no ordinary runaway horse he rode. This was yet another of his beggar girl's enchantments.

*

Violet supposed she should be grateful the prince wasn't sawing at her mouth with the reins or kicking her sides bloody. His breathless curses were sufficient to upset her, some of them so creative she'd never heard their like before.

"Pestilent nag," he hissed as they pounded deeper into the forest. Among the trees, the light was as green and shifting as if they'd plunged underneath the sea. "I'll have you sliced up for dog meat! I can't believe I considered forgiving you!"

This inspired a pang, but she truly couldn't force herself to slow down. She'd never felt so peculiar as when she clamped the fairy's gold bit between her teeth and her body began to shift. Now her heart hammered like a horse's, and her thoughts were but half human. Dangers she didn't understand drove her onward, the instinct to flee overwhelming her. Being strong and fast wasn't the fun she'd imagined when the fairy first described it.

It wasn't fun at all when Augustin sagged forward in exhaustion and simply clung to her.

She wasn't certain, but she thought he might be weeping a little.

At last, as the day's sun melted into orange and crimson behind the trees, Violet's weary legs stopped running. The prince slid from her and hit the ground like a sack.

He rolled onto his back, groaning to God in a way that was not a prayer. With his weight gone from her saddle, she remembered how to spit out the enchanted bit.

Her body changed in a twinkling. One moment, she stood on four quivering legs. The next, she toppled forward off two.

"I hate you," said the prince, his tone venomous though no louder than a ghost's. "More than I thought it possible for me to."

Violet lay flat on her face. Somehow she managed to turn her head to him.

If she'd had the breath, she'd have gasped. Stripes of blood, too numerous to count, crisscrossed the prince's upper body. A few scraps of material stuck to the wounds, as if his shirt and leather jerkin had been whipped off. Cold horror spread through her. A whipping was exactly what he'd endured.

"The pine branches," she said. "They must have been hitting you all along."

"Oh, not all along," the prince contradicted, mustering a smidgen of sarcasm. "If it had been *all* along, I'm sure I'd just be dead."

Violet pushed herself up to sit. "I'm so sorry, Augustin. So, so very sorry. A fairy told me to abduct you."

"And you had to listen?" Augustin laid one welted forearm across his eyes. "I thought you liked me."

A single tear squeezed from beneath the corner of his closed eyelid, rolling directly into his matted hair. Violet's heart clenched so tightly she truly thought it would break. She sensed he wouldn't have admitted this if he weren't utterly worn down.

"I *do* like you," she swore. "More than like you. You are a gallant knight. Any other man would be trying to kill me now."

"Too tired for that," her prince sighed.

Guilt was an effective energizer. Violet jumped up, swayed, then looked down at Augustin.

"Stay there," she said stupidly. "I think I heard running water up ahead."

She'd smelled it, actually, but that seemed funny to say.

When she reached the fern-shrouded brook, she realized she had nothing with which to carry back a drink for him. She was stark naked but for her hair, which her braid just barely contained. The fact that she took so long to notice she wore no clothes suggested she wasn't herself quite yet.

Thwarted in her purpose, she returned to bring the prince to the brook. He didn't want her to assist him and wearily told her to leave him alone. Ignoring his protests, she slung his big arm around her shoulders and helped him, hobbling and cursing, to the water.

"You're naked," he grumbled as she let his weight down so he could sit.

Violet pressed her lips together. Nice of him to notice. "You're not dressed for a fete yourself."

He narrowed his eyes at her before bending over the water to wash himself. Cleansing off the blood revealed numerous cuts and bruises, but thankfully his condition was not as bad as she'd feared.

"I heal fast," he said curtly, noting her expression. "I have a fairy godmother. When I was a child, she blessed me with good looks and vitality. Her husband threw in an untiring sword. That's what makes me a superior champion."

"I imagine it's not the only thing that does."

He shot her another suspicious glance. "If I take a sword cut, it heals in minutes. Any damage from a man- or fae-made weapon, I pretty much shrug off."

Was he trying to deny he was brave?

"You're not impervious to harm," she said, gesturing to his welts.

"No," he admitted, then winced as he tried to pick a piece of linen out of a deeper slash.

"Let me. Your hands are still trembling."

He sighed but dropped his muscular arms, scooting around so she could reach the injuries on his chest. The piece of shirt he'd been attempting to remove was caught in a cut above his left nipple. Violet struggled not to notice how the flat disk sharpened when she poured a cupped palm of water over it. Augustin didn't flinch as she carefully pulled the stuck threads free. Her breast swayed against his bicep. She knew she was breathing raggedly, but that wasn't something she could prevent.

Bojik's curse had woken with a vengeance inside of her.

"My God," the prince whispered. "Your beauty would try a saint."

When she looked, his gaze was locked on her nipples. Their aroused state was much more noticeable than his. The prince's diaphragm moved faster, his lips parted for his breathing, a hill slowly lifting the wet cloth of his trousers. The sight of his cock stretching mesmerized her. Violet shuddered, her sex clenching. Augustin's eyes rose and hers did too. His golden hair was slicked back from washing up, his face too starkly handsome for his looks to qualify as *good*. Beads of water from the brook sparkled on his high cheekbones. She saw herself reflected in his swollen black pupils.

"*I'm* not beautiful," she said.

"No?" His smile was almost too faint to see. Suddenly, she felt his hand on her breast, warmly cupping the pulsing curve. "You feel beautiful to me."

Violet had been kneeling, thighs together, naked bottom propped on her heels. When his callused palm compressed and turned on her nipple, hot creamy moisture ran out of her.

Augustin's nostrils flared, his gaze dropping to her mouth. Unable to stop herself, Violet wet it and leaned forward.

"Don't kiss me, sorceress," he said.

She jerked back and he let her, though his hold remained on her breast. In truth, he didn't seem able to loosen it. He glowered at that, clearly displeased with the stubbornness of his hand. He thought wanting her would harm him. Violet's eyes stung with hurt. She'd rather he didn't see this reaction, but of course he did.

"Oh, hell," he said and leaned in to kiss her himself.

His firm smooth lips pressed hers with a sigh. Violet let out a matching sound and pressed back. Any resistance either of them might have managed burned away in the immediate flare of heat.

Even as he pushed her body back to the ground, Augustin undid his trousers. Her mouth opened for him and then her legs. To her relief, he didn't hesitate to fill that cradle. His pelvis made a wonderful swiveling motion, working his thick bare length in between her folds. Violet moaned at how good that felt. He had one arm crooked behind her head, pillowing her neck. His other hand caressed her bottom, then coaxed her thigh to bend around his hip. His tongue slid slowly, deeply into her mouth, his hand leaving her leg to glide up and cup her breast. His fingers tightened until their tips pinched one tight nipple.

Sensation shot from that point of pressure along deeply buried nerves, causing her engorged clit to burn like it was on fire. Violet writhed, and the prince's teeth caught her lower lip. She wouldn't have thought she'd like being nipped, but she did. He licked the little sore place after, pulling a pleasured whimper into her throat. When he drew back, his eyes burned like twin blue flames.

"Put your arms around me," he said, the harshness of his instruction rasping her eardrum.

"I'm afraid I'll hurt you."

"Do it anyway."

She did it, and he let out a groan so rife with sexual enjoyment that she couldn't be sorry if she bothered his injuries. Held in her arms, he hitched hips against her in short but powerful motions, repeatedly driving his erection up and down her a few inches. It was enough to make any girl lose control, and Violet was hardly *any* girl.

"Be still," he said, the fingers that trapped her nipple tugging deliciously. "I'm going to rub my prick over your best spots. If you keep thrashing, you'll interfere with my aim."

She tried to obey him, but her spine arched up. God, she wanted him to drive inside her, to fill her aching pussy with that smooth rock-hard heat. The intensity of the longing was sufficient to make her speak. "You can't put your cock inside me."

"I know." He growled it, sounding a bit angry.

"It isn't just that I'm a virgin. My fairy warned me we'd both go mad if you did."

"As opposed to how sane I'm feeling now?" He cursed and rocked faster, his hand now clamped on her bottom, keeping her exactly where he wanted. Since he'd traded kissing her for breathing, she could see the veins on his neck. They stood out sharply, muscles straining as he ground himself into her. Arousing as this was to watch, it wasn't the strongest source of her excitement.

The flare of his penis was strafing her swollen pearl, pushing the hood off and on each time he dragged over it. Sensations built within her, each one better than the last. He was so thick he really spread her labia. Eager to urge him closer, Violet slid her hands down his back to his hindquarters. These muscles were as strong as the rest of him, compact and rounded as only a fit man's could be. Their skin was velvety, the lash marks from the trees stopping at his waist. She couldn't seem to resist pulling his cheeks apart.

Augustin grunted when her fingertips found the tight pleats around his hole. She traced the whorl and pushed curiously at it. Moisture that wasn't hers sluiced from his cock onto her. She wasn't certain, but she thought his shaft had just jerked longer.

"Do you like that?" she asked breathlessly. "Sometimes, when I'm pleasuring myself, I like to push something into me from behind."

"Christ," he said, but he wasn't cursing in disapproval. He grabbed her hand and wedged it between their rubbing groins. "Wet your fingers. I want at least three of them shoved in me."

Oh, what he did to her with his orders! She let him coat her fingers in her juices, then put her hand back where it had been. Afraid to take him completely at his word, she pushed two past his tight entrance.

"No," he said harshly, his head dipping down to hers. "Don't be so careful. Give me what I asked for."

She kept her eyes on his as she did, wanting to be sure she didn't hurt him. His pupils expanded and his breath sucked in. His passage was smooth as satin and very hot, easing around her as she pushed three fingers past the first tight inches.

"That's it." His voice was suddenly deeper, as if his chest had loosened with enjoyment. "Rub me all the way in and out. I like that the same way you do."

He exhaled in pleasure as she gently pumped, his hips starting to roll into her again. That felt as good as before, but Violet had a new goal in mind.

"There's a spot I heard about," she panted. "Only men are supposed to have it. I don't think my fingers are long enough to reach."

The prince's nearly silent chuckle shook his broad shoulders. "I know the one, princess." He moved his left knee up and to the side, scooting her farther down him at the same time. "Try to reach now."

She knew when she found the place because his spine stiffened like a bow and his penis pressed into her so hard she had at least half an orgasm.

He groaned something that might have been *again*. Violet decided she ought to do the same thing faster and harder. That's what she'd have wanted in his position.

The prince seemed to agree with her choice. Proving himself more limber than she expected, he arched to her and sealed his mouth over the peak of one breast. His tongue and lips felt even better than his fingers. Hot gold wires stretched inside her as he suckled. She gave a cry and came all the way.

He moaned with her in his mouth, his pull on her nipple as basic as a child's. Sophisticated reactions must have been beyond him. She continued to pump her fingers, working that extra gift from Eros as steadily as she could.

Finally, it was too much.

"Fuck," he gasped, his eyes squeezing shut as his big body heaved closer. "*Augh.*"

Heat spurted up her belly at that last cry, three forceful jets that somehow drove her excitement higher. When the last jet ceased, Augustin pushed carefully off her, hanging over her on his hands and knees. Like her, he was breathing hard.

"Did I hurt you?" he asked.

She shook her head. Her hand had pulled free when he rose from her. The way he was breathing—and *flushing*—made her curl it into a fist.

"That was good," he said, his voice so gravelly she shivered. "You made me come very strongly. You have a gift for pleasing a man."

Violet's nipples were hard as diamonds, throbbing violently at his words. Augustin's gaze drifted down to them. A shadow moved beneath his belly, his recently pleasured cock stiffening. She sensed him fighting a groan.

"I want more too," she blurted in confession.

*

She was going to kill him. He should have been offended by the thought that her lust was magically wound up. Pride dictated that a woman's desire to swive him ought to be due to him. Rather than put him off, however, her affliction strengthened by tenfold the other reasons he wanted her. It had taken every shred of control he had not to shove his cock into her pussy a hundred times. The very idea obsessed him. To push himself into that tightness, to feel her juice creaming around him . . .

Augustin shuddered, his back teeth grinding at the yearning that rose in him. She was too good a match for him. Walking away was no longer an option.

"Sit up," he grated out. "Then turn around on your hands and knees."

He had to shift back so she could move. He was painfully hard again, his erection thudding up vertical from his groin. Helpless not to touch it, he wrapped one hand around the base and squeezed.

Violet paused mid-turn, her eyes widening at what he was doing. "You're so beautiful," she breathed. "If it were possible for me to take you . . ."

His prick hardened until it stung, fluid rolling warm from its hole. She thought this beast of his beautiful? "Violet, get into position *now*."

She understood what he meant. She pushed her gorgeous ass in the air, bracing her upper body on her forearms. The pose was better than he'd asked for: knees spread, glistening pussy on display. The serpent's apple could not have been this tempting. Her sex was rosy and pulsing with her desire. Arched as she was, the pouting nipples of her breasts nearly brushed the ground.

He swallowed, reminding himself she wasn't trying to ensnare him. She trusted him to control himself.

"Violet," he groaned, moving over her. "I'm just going to touch my tip to your entrance. I want to be sure I'm wet enough."

They shivered in unison at the contact. She was so hot, and the little mouth kissed at him.

"Augustin—"

"I know." He pressed his sensitive tip ever so gently into the heat of her. "You feel so nice. Just give me a few seconds."

"Please." Her hips wriggled as she begged, arousing him insanely. "I can't stand it. If you stay there, I'll beg you to come inside."

She welled around him, and he had to tilt his head back to gasp for air. Every particle of his being screamed for him to drive into that sweet wetness.

"All right," he panted, somehow finding the will to drag himself from the brink. "I'm backing away now."

She whimpered as he moved his slickened crown to her anus, but the sound was neither fear nor pain. Knowing she wanted him this intensely drew a rumble of lust from him. He bent around her, one hand swallowing her pubis while the other planted on the soft moss in front of her. Her long red braid had fallen forward over her shoulder, baring her nape to him. He nuzzled her vertebrae, loving her delicacy here, how it marked her as feminine. His lips opened in a kiss, his tongue licking salt from her skin. With the oddest sense that he was falling from a great height, he pressed his crown past that first ring of snug muscle.

"Oh God," she gasped, one hand fumbling back for his hip. "Augustin, don't stop there."

Humor curved his mouth as he pushed in slowly; she was no timider about this act than he was. When he'd penetrated about two inches, he withdrew the knob to just within her entrance. He knew what she was feeling: how every nerve prickled with delight, how the forbidden heat spread and tugged other places she wouldn't think could be connected.

His knowledge of her pleasure heightened his. Sweat rolled down him as he took her in small nudges, ecstasy sparking through his penis even as he tried to make each motion as pleasurable for her as he could. He didn't think he'd ever been this gentle. She was so little, so tight, and the last thing he wanted was to hurt her. Luckily, his body was making more lubrication, drop after drop of silky precum welling excitedly from his slit. He set a rhythm with his hand on the front of her, rubbing up and down, then circling, then squeezing her labia to her clit and rolling all three strongly together. He suspected this wasn't a trick she did for herself. That she liked it he couldn't doubt. Her pearl swelled to a size and firmness that enraptured him. She came the second time he compressed her folds around it.

After that, everything was easy.

Her body relaxed enough that he could stroke almost all the way in and out. He was still careful, but now he was climbing the hill with her, those sparks of pleasure no longer separate from each other. Now they accumulated, building toward a peak he suspected would be immense. Violet's moans told him she longed to scale the heights as well. Their mutual rise felt amazing, a challenge they surmounted together. He made noises like she was killing him, but the truth could have been the opposite. It felt like life she brought him, more and more of it stuffing into his soul. His balls pulled tight, the need to spill spiking in his loins. He groaned at the realization that he didn't have to pull out this time. He could shoot the flood that was gathering into her.

"Yes," she urged, her voice breathy. "Yes, I'm as close as you."

"A few more thrusts," he said, barely able to form the words. "A few . . . Oh Lord, you feel so *good.*"

She felt like satin, vised around every sensitive blazing inch. Only her pussy could have been better. Wanting her to feel just as good, he gave her mons the rolling squeeze she'd proved so fond of.

She moaned and a moment later gushed over his fingers. Her reaction was a match struck to dry tinder. He didn't need to thrust. Her body tightened on him and tugged him into the gulf whose brink he'd been teetering on. He felt the heat of his seed rushing from his tip, felt her quiver and come again. That made him spill harder, his climax expanding and strengthening and suddenly becoming so intense he thought he understood what made his bed partners swoon.

Violet didn't swoon. Violet let out a sound so close to a scream that his throat simply had to roar in answer.

She'd pulled another climax from him, before the previous peak finished. At last, his shaft drove all the way into her, balls shoved tight to her round bottom. Relief besieged him, fresh seed jetting from him in cannon bursts.

"Oh . . . my," she groaned, then "*God*" on a new spasm.

He didn't know how long they held there, straining to each other as luscious aftershocks ran through them. Long minutes certainly. He didn't collapse, but he wanted to.

When he pulled out, she looked about to buckle. Augustin caught her before she could.

"Let me help you wash. We look like we've been rolling in a mud puddle."

The brook felt even icier after they'd been so warm. Violet could have rinsed herself, but he liked doing it. Though he'd touched many women, she fascinated him. Her combination of tininess and ripe curves was different from anyone he'd caressed. He let his hands drink their fill, stroking her arms, her breasts, the adorable dip of her navel. When his thumb drew down the wet meeting of her thighs, Violet looked up at him.

Her eyes were olive beneath the trees, her lashes a dark lush red. Again, he had that sense that he was falling. His cock twitched, reminding him it could rise again. Violet's hand lifted to his face, slender fingers brushing his lower lip. His mouth tingled as she did.

"Augustin," she murmured.

Every day, he thought. *I want to hear her say my name like that every day.*

He cleared his throat, abruptly uncomfortable. "You need clothes."

One corner of her mouth jerked up.

"I know. Any sensible man would leave you naked. I would myself most days. I'm just concerned your people will throw me in the stocks if I bring you home this way."

"You're . . . bringing me home?"

Her lips had gone round. Augustin let his breath out on a low sigh. He had a feeling he'd regret this. In fact, he was pretty sure what he said next would be his afterglow talking.

"I'm going to defeat your were-wolf for you."

"Oh Augustin. Your highness!" She clasped her hands together before her breasts, her beautiful eyes bright with gratitude.

"I'm being practical," he said, striving for a dismissive tone. "If I don't give in, who knows how you'll torture me next!"

Chapter 9

T hey'd already crossed the border into Arnwall. The prince
slipped out of the woods alone, returning a short while later
with suitable if not fancy garments for her. Violet dragged the shirt
and kirtle on gratefully, possibly a bit too conscious of Augustin
watching.

"Stole them off a clothes line," he said. "You owe one of your
tenants."

His tone was brusque, as if acceding to her wishes irritated him.
Unsure of his mood and not wanting to say something to change his
mind, Violet kept her mouth shut as they tramped side by side up the
coastal road. A dull sweet ache pulsed in her back passage, but she did
her best not to dwell on those sensations. Wallowing in arousal
wouldn't sharpen her wits.

She knew the prince was taking in his surroundings: the newly
turned fields, the tidy but weathered dwellings, the occasional peasant
clopping by in a cart. An hour into their journey, they stopped at a
rocky overlook by the beach. A boat lay overturned on the sand
below, its silvered hull awaiting repair.

Augustin's deep blue eyes squinted out to sea, his hands clasped
calmly behind him. He hadn't stolen a shirt for himself, and the
smoothly hewn expanse of his back was bare. Whatever had inspired
his earlier anger, he'd released it. Together they watched the sun
sparkle off the waves.

Violet couldn't help remembering the naked seal king with her
pretty mother slung over his huge shoulder, his big male hand
caressing her bottom as he held her in place. Worse, she remembered
how her father—who'd been dragged off first and was farther out in
the water—had ceased struggling in his captors' grip as the king
approached. Her father's handsome face had gone flushed and dazed,
his lips slack with shock. At the time, Violet hadn't recognized the
expression. Now she wished she could erase her knowledge of what
it was. Her father, the King of Arnwall, had been aroused at his

kidnapping.

Violet jerked as Augustin cleared his throat, pulling her from her reverie. She hoped her thoughts weren't showing. She'd told no one of her suspicions, and had no intention of changing that.

"Fishing is good here?" Augustin asked.

"It's better than some places. Most years our fishermen make a good living."

He nodded, his profile so finely carved his face could have graced a coin. "They may be alive," he said, his compatible turn of thought causing her to blink in surprise. "You shouldn't give up hope. Stranger things have happened."

"Wherever they are, I pray they're together. They loved each other very much."

He turned to her, and her stomach dipped, the ground beneath her seeming to drop a foot. She realized she could love this man. With his gaze so quiet and steady, he seemed a rock in an upheaved world. It didn't matter to her heart that he helped her reluctantly. She knew then that what he promised, he would fulfill. *His* word would be his bond.

She looked away before the sting behind her eyes rose to their surface.

"We should go on," she said. "I've been away long enough."

They encountered the first dead cow two miles short of her castle. The carcass lay in a ditch, intestines gutted, heart missing from its chest. A cloud of flies rose at their approach, but the beast hadn't been dead long.

Prince Augustin stopped, looked down at the remains, then took her hand and pulled her gently away.

A second cow sprawled across the road further on, followed shortly by two sheep. The last still held a mouthful of clover between its teeth.

"This is just savagery," the prince said grimly. "He's barely eaten them."

"It's a message. To me, I expect. To torment me on my return."

The prince's fingers tightened around hers. "His wolf does not rule him then. Messages are the province of men."

Violet couldn't disagree. Her throat was too clenched for speech anyway.

A smaller shape, this one brown with white spots, lay curled under a pasture wall. Violet recognized it as the blacksmith's dog. Tidbit was friendly creature, no taller than her knee, a pet to many in the village. More than once she'd seen Bojik toss sticks to it to retrieve.

"Bojik, *no*," she murmured before she could stop herself. If he'd done this, he was truly lost.

Tidbit lifted his head and barked.

The dog wasn't dead. It had only been sleeping. The depth of her relief astounded her. Was she honestly holding out hope that Bojik was redeemable?

"Well, well," sneered a voice so low and gravelly it stood all her hairs on end. "Arnwall's fair ruler condescends to return. And it looks like she's brought a friend."

Violet's tormentor had been hiding in the branches of a broad thorn tree. He dropped lightly to his feet as he spoke. His brown eyes glowed with uncanny light, his fingernails transformed into claws. He wasn't the man she'd left a few days ago. Then he could have been mistaken for a true suitor. Now, despite his smirk, the energy he radiated was dark and unhappy. He was dirty too, which he never had been before.

Steel rasped softly as Prince Augustin withdrew a blade from his boot.

Bojik's grin bared incisors that had grown inhuman. "Ah, Princess Violet's little friend has a stinger. This is going to be fun."

Violet shot a glance at her champion, painfully aware that he wore no mail or armor—or even a linen shirt. The knife he'd pulled was long but far shorter than a sword. At least he held it like he knew what to do with it. His face was perfectly serene, his body crouched—for defense or attack, she supposed.

"I'm big enough to take you," he said.

Augustin was taller than Bojik but not as brawny. Bojik laughed, and the men began to circle each other, scuffing up puffs of dirt on the dusty road. Though it was midday, no traffic stirred. Violet suspected her people were giving this cow-strewn thoroughfare a wide berth.

"Bojik," she said, willing her voice to remain steady. "We should talk before we do this."

Bojik ignored her, his glowing eyes fastened on Augustin. "Did she open her thighs for you, Goldilocks? Did you stick your little stinger into her cunt?"

Rather than deny it, Augustin smiled at him.

Bojik roared, brown wolf hair washing up his strong arms in waves. He dove toward Augustin with his claws outstretched. If he hadn't been so outraged, he probably would have gored the prince with them.

Fortunately, Augustin was nimble. He ducked away from the leap, obliging Bojik to hit the dirt and roll. He was up in an instant, facing Augustin a smidgen more warily. Violet's breath sucked in as she got a look at Bojik. He was half wolf now, his face lengthened by a muzzle, his furry chest so large it had torn the leather laces on his jerkin.

Apparently, Augustin was less impressed.

"Woof-woof," he mocked, his knife ready before him. "Come and get it, doggy."

Goading Bojik to lose his temper seemed a reasonable tactic, except an angry were-wolf was no ordinary opponent. This time Bojik charged the prince too fast to avoid. Because his strength was unnatural, his upward momentum carried both men over the pasture wall. They hit the sparse grass beyond with a series of tumbling thuds.

Violet heard a wolflike yelp, then a decidedly human cry of pain. At that, she absolutely could not stop herself from running to the wall to see what was happening.

She discovered the men on their feet again, each one's hands clamped around the other's throat. They seemed to be trying to push each other off balance. If the prince's neck hadn't been leaking thick red streams around the were-wolf's claws, Violet might have thought them equally matched.

The sight of her champion bleeding jolted her heart up into her throat. A were-wolf's claws weren't forged weapons, and they could harm Augustin. From the looks of the fan of red sliding down his chest, he probably could be killed.

"She's mine," Bojik snarled, the claim distorted by his wolf mouth. "No other man can love her as I do."

Augustin grunted, his rear heel skidding backward on the grass. "A flea-bitten stray could love her better than you."

Bojik's arms exploded with a massive shove. Taken unprepared, Augustin's feet slid out from under him. He tumbled back and Violet screamed, terror an icy fire in her veins. Bojik had the prince at his mercy. His giant malformed frame fell on him . . .

And then, against all logic, *he* howled with pain. He was flying over Augustin's head. He landed curled into a ball and retching. It seemed Augustin had driven both his boots full force to his testicles.

Augustin sprang onto his feet before the were-wolf could recover, his knees looking wobbly but strong enough. As quickly as he could, he searched the grass for his fallen knife, grabbed it, and strode forward.

"Bastard," Bojik gasped, helpless to uncurl. "I *love* her. You tell me you can say as much."

Augustin's approach hesitated for one heartbeat. Violet's fingers dug into the stones of the pasture's wall. In that moment, she couldn't have said what she was most afraid of. Bojik's wolf features had receded, perhaps because of his pain. He looked young to her, barely a man at all.

"I'm sorry," Augustin said, his fist tightening on his knife. "I can't let that stop me from killing you."

"Do it then. I'd rather die than watch her love you."

He closed his eyes, and the prince's knife arm flashed up. Violet knew he would hit Bojik's heart. Her champion's aim was too sure and her enemy too resigned. Violet's palm clapped over her mouth.

God help him, she prayed—and she didn't mean the prince.

A snarling blur of brown and white streaked across the pasture as the blade descended. The blade thumped the center of Bojik's chest, sinking resonantly through flesh and bone. To her surprise, both the men cried out. In the confusion, Tidbit had attacked Augustin. The terrier was smart enough not to target the prince's boot. His jaw was clamped on his calf, his teeth holding his furry weight off the ground as Augustin tried to kick him loose.

"Don't!" Violet pleaded, scrambling over the wall. "Don't hurt him. He thinks Bojik is his friend. Bojik used to play with him."

Augustin put his boot down without flinging off the dog. His neck still bled where Bojik's claws had dug in, but Violet saw the holes were closing.

"Shh," she said, bending to put her hands on the furious animal. "Let go now. Everything is all right."

The dog relaxed as she petted it, dropping from Augustin with a whine. Violet was trembling from head to toe as she stood again. Augustin touched her shoulder, the eyes that met hers so somber she couldn't keep hers from welling up.

"So," said a shaky whispering laugh. "One sort of canine you will defend."

The whisper was Bojik's. Violet couldn't believe he was still alive. Everyone knew heart strikes were fatal to were-wolves. He lay on his back behind Augustin, legs drawn up slightly in pain. The knife was stuck in him to its hilt, the gory hand with which Bojik wrapped too feeble to wrench it out.

Violet thought nothing of dropping to her knees beside him. She laid her hand on his rapidly paling cheek.

He laughed raspingly again. "Don't know if I'll die or not. I think . . . my champion knocked your fellow's aim off a hair." He winced as blood trickled from his mouth. "You could give the dagger a final turn. That might be poetic."

"Oh Bojik. Why couldn't you let me go? Why did you have to turn violent?"

"It's my nature," he said. A tear fell from her face onto his. He blinked as it hit him, something that could have been remorse flickering through his expression. "I'm sorry, princess. I shouldn't have hurt you."

"*I* could have borne it. You shouldn't have hurt my people."

Her sudden anger sent a flinch through him. She didn't know if he understood, nor why it mattered to her.

"Violet." Augustin's hand brushed against her hair. "Do you want me to finish him?"

Did she have a choice? Bojik was a monster. He'd become a danger to her people. Her rejection might have played a part in his descent, but it was he who'd decided how to respond.

Augustin met her questioning eyes gravely. "He is your subject, princess. You have the right to pronounce his sentence."

"He might die even if we pull out the knife."

"Yes," Augustin agreed.

She looked back at Bojik. Could he change? Did he want to? She couldn't read what was in his face aside from pain and perhaps a shadow of fear for death. Whatever he felt, she knew he was too proud to beg for mercy.

"We could leave you to God," she said. "See if He wishes to spare you."

Bojik shifted uneasily. "Princess—"

"I ask no vows." Her tone as she interrupted was hard as stone.

"Your word means nothing to me, but I hope you know I mean mine. If you survive your wound, you must leave Arnwall and not return. If we ever—and I do mean *ever*—hear of you wreaking havoc elsewhere, Prince Augustin and myself will immediately hunt you down. Make your choice, Bojik. Do I remove the knife, or do I give it—as you put it—a final poetic turn?"

Bojik's eyes had widened, her resolute manner startling him. He licked dry lips, tasting his heart blood as he did so.

"Pull it out," he whispered. "God or the devil take me as they desire."

Chapter 10

A ugustin knew he should be reveling in triumph. He'd defeated a deadly were-wolf. He'd rescued a fair princess. Her people were at that moment feting him in their banquet hall. He simply couldn't enjoy the accolades. Bojik's words circled through his mind like a hoop rolling down a hill.

I love her. You tell me you can say as much.

"To the Prince of Madrigar," toasted yet another of Violet's courtiers. The well-dressed older man had risen from his seat, his drinking cup held aloft. "We cannot thank him enough for saving Arnwall's most precious possession."

They had no idea what a treasure she really was. The prince looked at her, sitting by his side at the high table, smiling quietly. She was dressed befitting her station in rich pink velvet slashed with chartreuse, her glorious red hair held up with pearl pins. An endearing blush adorned her low neckline, the modesty the blush suggested at odds with the passion he knew her to be capable of. He'd been stone hard from his first glimpse of her in the gown, his erection scarcely contained by his borrowed tights and codpiece. If he lived an eternity, he would not forget the incredible sense of aliveness she made him feel.

Squirming on his hard high-backed chair, he thought back to how she'd freed Bojik from the knife that impaled his heart. She'd refused the prince's help, planting her slipper on the were-wolf's chest and pulling back so firmly she did him no further harm. She'd been as white as a ghost, but she had not quailed. If Bojik lived, it would be thanks to her courage and compassion. If he died—which he might; they'd left him bleeding and near a faint in the field—he knew she'd shoulder her part in that as well.

Augustin didn't think he'd ever met a woman so fit to rule.

"To Arnwall's jewel," someone else cried out. "May she always grace us with her beauty!"

"I have something to say."

The words came from Augustin. Though he hadn't planned to rise, he was on his feet, his chased silver chalice lifted before him. Its rim was dented, as was much of Arnwall's silver. He pushed that thought aside as the hall quieted for him. A hint of heat touched his cheeks, informing him he was flushed. Since he couldn't quash the reaction, he pretended it wasn't there.

"First," he said. "I thank you for your kind welcome. My own people could not have received me more graciously. However—" He paused to send his gaze around the crowded tables, letting his caveat sink in. "I marvel to hear you praise me for my courage and the princess only for her beauty. That she is a beauty I don't deny, but she is no 'jewel,' no 'possession' to simply sit up here and sparkle.

"For many months, while a dangerous beast assailed her, *she* turned his wrath from you. That more of you have not suffered losses is due to her. When she could keep the monster at bay no longer, it was this tiny maid, this woman barely out of girlhood, who left to seek aid for you. Worse, she sought it alone. None of you tried to fight Bojik, nor did any brave the perils she did to find someone to rescue you. I wonder, just a little, whether you deserve to be defended by a girl as valiant as your princess."

Silence reigned in the aftermath of his speech, jaws hanging open around the room.

"Augustin," Violet murmured, clearly embarrassed.

Before she could object to his defense, one young man jumped to his feet at a near table. "The prince is right! We owe the princess our deepest apologies."

Hand over heart, he threw himself to one knee more theatrically than some might say was required. Since a dozen others shortly joined him, Augustin forgave him. Before a hundred hearts had beaten a hundred times, every soul in the room was offering obeisance to her.

"Please," Violet objected. "You needn't do this. I love you all. It is my privilege to serve."

To Augustin's delight, not a one of her subjects stirred. Violet blushed furiously as he tugged her onto her feet. Inside, he was grinning. Outside, he bowed over her small white hand with all the chivalry he possessed.

"Your highness," he said, pressing a soft kiss to her fingers.

He didn't mean for his lips to linger, but they did anyway. This might be the last time he clasped her hand in his.

Her fingers trembled and then grew hot. With all these people watching, she wanted him. Augustin bit back a groan at the tidal wave of lust that crashed over him. If only he could have kept her. If only he could have given her the adoring, faithful heart she deserved.

When he straightened, his vision was dangerously blurred.

"Princess," he said, his voice throbbing, "knowing you has been an honor and a joy."

He saw her startled hurt as he stepped past her. He knew she didn't expect him to leave, not in the middle of a banquet, not after everything he'd just said. He couldn't help that. He had to go while he had the strength.

I'm sorry, he thought, ordering his feet to walk on. *If I weren't broken, I'd stay with you forever.*

*

As soon as she could depart without causing comment, Violet escaped to Arnwall's chapel. Shaking with relief and sorrow, she slipped into the second of its ten pews. Here the walls were stone clad, the solitary stained glass window above the altar showing a kneeling warrior being knighted by his king. The king was Violet's great grandfather, the source of her vivid hair. Faint rays of moonlight glimmered through his gold crown. He'd been a godly man, she had heard, and a fearless soldier.

Violet thought that side of him would have admired Augustin.

Her sudden sob choked her throat, the tears that followed hot and numerous. Augustin's departure shouldn't have caught her unprepared like this. What did she have to offer him, after all? Her kingdom was paltry when set beside the one he'd inherit. As for her, she was barely pretty, no matter what the prince was princely enough to say. If she was clever, she wasn't clever enough to have kept Arnwall out of trouble, plus she'd treated Augustin horribly. It was ridiculous to think he'd forgive her, to hope he'd return her feelings.

Though she was sure he meant well by defending her tonight, he'd reminded her she was alone. Bojik had been right on that score. Sad as it was to admit, with her parents gone, the only person who loved her with all his being was a monster.

Her tears fell faster, her nose soon clogged. She dug in her gown's hidden pocket for her silk handkerchief.

"Tut-tut," said a musical voice as she covered her nose and blew.

"What's all this weeping for?"

A lovely woman sat beside her on the old pew, her beautiful flaxen hair foaming in waves to her waist. Violet was certain she hadn't heard her come in.

"Pardon?" she croaked, hoarse from crying. "Do I know you?"

The woman smiled. "How soon you humans forget. We met in the Wailing Woods. My raven led you safely to Madrigar."

"The fairy!" Violet exclaimed, coloring up as she remembered what she'd been doing before they met. "I thought you were old."

"I *am*, child, compared to you."

The fairy's high spirits pricked Violet's anger. "You made me hurt Augustin."

"Did I?" The fairy tilted her lovely head. "Are you certain he's not better off than he was before? Some people need to have a little hurt whipped in them. Only then do they discover what they're made of."

Violet opened her mouth to argue, and then decided she'd better not. The fairy was a powerful magic being and—as Augustin himself had observed—no one had forced Violet to listen to what she'd said.

"Such a scowl!" the fairy scolded, her humor undimmed by it. "Would it make you feel better if you knew I was his fairy godmother?"

"Good Lord," Violet burst out. "I'd hate to see what you'd do if you were his enemy."

The fairy laughed some more, then wiped a few twinkling tears from her sea green eyes. "Fairies look at ends, my dear. Means rarely concern them. Do you remember what I promised you: that my solution would not lead you to misery?"

Violet's response was stiffer than she intended. "Forgive me, but I cannot see as you've fulfilled that."

"Only because you don't see as far I do. You give up too soon, little girl. You haven't walked the whole road I've set you on." The fairy shook her finger, then bent to her, pressing her perfect lips to the center of Violet's brow. Violet smelled spring flowers and heard a glissando of tiny harps. The fairy drew back, her green eyes glowing in a manner that reminded her of Bojik. Though Violet believed her to mean no harm, the fairy was more frightening than the were-wolf.

"Tell the prince Ariel sends him love," she said.

She winked out in a burst of sparkles before Violet could respond.

"Tell him yourself," she huffed, but she knew Ariel was right.

She could sit here pitying herself, or she could at least try to fight for her heart's desire.

*

The door to the guest chamber was ajar. Candles glowed inside, so Violet supposed the prince was there. Her hands were cold, her sex uncomfortably hot. It didn't care what sort of reception she might receive. It only knew the man who best matched its longings was near.

"Augustin?" she said, afraid to simply go in.

She heard a soft catch of breath. "Come," said Augustin's voice to her.

When she walked in, he wore his own dirty trousers. The clothes he'd been given to wear for the feast lay neatly folded on a chair beside the curtained four-poster bed. The prince turned to face her as if reluctant but unable to help himself. A muscle clenched in his jaw as their gazes met. His eyes were dark in the candlelight: sapphires in shadow.

"You're leaving." She'd known he would, but hurt still rode out with the statement.

"I must. The longer I stay, the harder it will be to go."

Violet nodded, her lips pressed tight. At least he found it difficult—not that this did her much good. She gestured toward the formal clothes. "You don't have to return those, though I suppose . . . They must not be as nice as what you're used to."

"They're fine," he said very firmly. "Perfect. The loan of them was extremely kind. *You* are extremely kind."

His golden brows drew together above his bladelike nose, his expression pleading for something—perhaps that she let him leave here without a scene. Violet crossed her arms underneath her breasts. "You can't go home in nothing but those trousers. Your people will think mine are rude."

"Then I'll take the shirt as well, if that pleases you."

"Augustin."

"Violet." He dropped his head in exasperation, one hand rubbing the back of his neck. "Believe me, if I could stay, I would."

"Just tell me what pulls you home. Another woman? Another monster you need to slay?"

"No. To both."

"Then I must have too few charms to entice you."

She'd said it haughtily, but he didn't react as she expected. He strode to her and took her arms, the groan that twisted from him sufficient to give her hope. His body blazed heat at her, her sex going liquid at the flush that rose up his chest. Unable to stop herself, she spread her hands across his muscled ribs. They, too, were hot as fire.

"Stay," she said, low and humble. "Do not let it end this way between us. If . . . if you're concerned you'd be trapped into marrying me, please accept my oath that I have no such designs. You're the only man I want to be with, but if you truly wish to go, I won't stop you."

"Vi-o-let," he growled, breaking her name apart. "You shouldn't be offering that to me."

Maybe she shouldn't, but she didn't care. If she spent one night with him and no more, she would cherish it all her life. His fingers tightened painfully on her arms. Violet rose on her toes and leaned in to him.

"Let me give this night to you. Let me thank you as you deserve. Even after all I put you through, you've been a true friend to me."

When he wagged his head, either denying it or disapproving, she pushed back from him. A moment was all she needed to pull the pearl-headed pins from her hair. The ankle-length red curtain fell in a silken rush. Augustin's hiss of response was the only sound louder.

"Don't." His voice was ragged, his hands curling into fists.

She stepped farther out of reach, wrenching the laces of her gown hard enough to snap. Freed, she shrugged all the layers she was wearing down to her waist. The chamber's air brushed her breasts. Augustin began to pant.

"You owe me nothing for this," she said, wanting to be crystal clear. "My kingdom isn't rich, but everything I am I give you freely."

She pushed the gown from her hips, letting it fall down her legs until she stood naked in the rich pool of cloth. Her hair hung loose behind her, left free so seldom the stir of it along her back felt strange. Augustin's gazed burned down her and up again, his chest rising and falling as swiftly as if he'd been running. He pressed one fist to his breastbone as if it hurt.

She imagined his cock was hurting. As his gaze fastened on her nipples, its arch pushed out his trousers like he had a tree branch in there.

"I dreamed this," he said so low it gave her chills. "I dreamed of you in nothing but your hair."

"If you tell me more dreams, I'll try to make them come true.

He shuddered. And swallowed. A wet spot appeared on the strained front of his trousers, no bigger than a penny but spreading. His prick was weeping for her. Her own body jerked with longing, a sympathetic trickle rolling from her labia.

"Violet," he rasped, finally meeting her eyes again. "Please God, Violet, *shut the door.*"

She'd forgotten it was ajar. Startled, she turned to push it completely shut.

The instant the iron latch clicked, his weight slammed her against the wood. His teeth nipped the tender back of her neck, his hands shoving up her front to clutch a pulsing breast in each palm. He was a big man, much taller and heavier than she. With muscles honed from at least a decade of fighting monsters, he had no trouble making her feel more helpless than she could have predicted she'd enjoy. He bent his knees and splayed them to even up their heights. When he ground a circle with his huge erection over her naked rear, another gush of cream squeezed from her.

"My God," he growled, hot against her nape. "Violet, you drive me insane."

He pushed the iron ridge in his trousers between her cheeks, squashing her slighter body into the wooden door. This was shockingly exciting, but not what she wanted most. She struggled to twist around.

"Please," she said when she found his weight wouldn't let her move.

Maybe he understood, or maybe he thought she was trying to escape and could not bear it. Either way, he eased back only enough for her to turn. Once she had, he caught her face in both hands, dropping his head to seal their mouths together in a blistering, lengthy kiss.

Violet doubted any kiss in the history of kissing had been this blatantly sexual. He penetrated her with his tongue, laying claim to every inch inside. He stroked her palate with the sleek sharpened tip. He rubbed the sides of their tongues together as if they were lower parts. He sucked her tongue into his mouth and moaned his ecstasy down her throat. When Violet sank her teeth into his lower lip and tugged, a tantalizing quiver shook the length of his spine.

"Vixen," he whispered, blue eyes agleam as his hands took her face more firmly.

He didn't seem disapproving. He seemed aroused. She thought he'd start up the kiss again, maybe more deeply. To her amazement, he screwed his eyes shut and stepped determinedly back from her.

"What is it?" she asked, rendered so breathless by his kiss that she wasn't sure he could hear. "Why do you stop?"

Augustin sighed and opened his eyes. His expression was more serious than she could view happily.

"Violet," he said, "as much as I'd love to accept your . . . truly stunning offer, there's something you need to know about me first."

"Yes?" Violet said. Seeing that whatever it was was difficult for him to speak of, she laid her fingertips very gently atop his diaphragm. It jerked with the ragged breath he drew in.

"Violet, I have no heart."

"No heart!" He frowned at her, so perhaps she shouldn't have sounded so disbelieving. "Augustin, I don't see how that's possible."

*

Of course she didn't believe him. A person couldn't walk around without an actual heart. Sadly, he knew too well there was more to that organ than a beating bundle of muscle.

"It's a magical lack," he said. "My mother accidentally angered a powerful fairy, who cursed me before my birth. Whatever it is that allows human beings to love, I am bereft of it. That bastard Bojik could offer you more devotion. The hell of it is—" He struggled not to betray the sudden awful wrenching inside his chest. It felt like his ribs were cracking, but he owed her this truth. "The hell of it is I'm relatively certain I love you anyway."

"Augustin." Though her eyes were kind, her breath came out on a snort.

"Don't laugh at me. You've no idea how much this hurts. Never really understanding what other people feel. Never being worth what they are, no matter how terrible they are. You deserve a whole man, not a shell like me."

"I've never met anyone who was less a shell."

He could see she meant it. Her sincerity shone from her. He swallowed, not wanting to say the words he felt honor bound to utter. "I'm not sure I'm capable of fidelity."

This at last gave her pause. "Is . . . is there someone else you want more than me?"

"No!" he cried, the assurance raw. "Only you. Since we met, no one else has appealed to me." The heart he'd never thought useful for more than pumping blood stuttered in his chest. A sense of marvel spread out from it. He hadn't wanted anyone but her, not the breakfast maid, not the beautiful princesses of Llyr. "That's never happened to me before." Maybe his impulsive words had been true. Maybe he did love her. The problem was he knew he was flawed. Loving her in spite of that wasn't good enough for her. He cupped the side of her upturned face, her cheek like velvet against his palm. "I don't think I could bear it if I ended up hurting you."

Violet put her hand over his, her thumb sweeping gently along its side. The tingles this sent streaking to his cock were a distraction he didn't need. He forced himself to focus on her answer.

"I love you," she said. In spite of everything, this kicked a thrill so strongly through him his knees threatened to buckle. "I have a heart that loves and admires you almost more than I can express. Even so—" She stopped a moment to pat his chest. "Even with my heart, I cannot promise I'll never cause you pain. That isn't what love is, at least not that I've seen."

He'd never searched a pair of eyes as he searched hers then. Could she be saying what he thought? "Would you take me then? As I am? Knowing I might fall short of what you deserve?"

"You don't fall short, Augustin. Someday I pray you'll know that as unshakably as I do."

Tears welled up in his eyes. He tried to blink them away, but a few spilled over. She smiled and tiptoed up to kiss him, her arms wrapping him tightly.

Augustin groaned and embraced her back. He meant to be gentle, but that just wasn't possible. She'd moved him too deeply. He ducked his head and kissed her like a starving man, eager hands sliding under her flaming hair.

Oh, how she humbled him. His desire spiraled upward as her hands roved his skin, the sounds she groaned into his kiss blessedly hungry. She loosed his trousers with frantic fingers, pushing them and his underthings down his legs. They were naked together then, nothing between him and the consummation that obsessed him.

When both her hands curled around and stroked his erection, no force on earth could have kept his hoarse cry inside.

"Take me," she said. "Be the only man I remember."

Did she honestly think he'd leave after this? That he would take her to bed and not to wife?

"Violet—"

"Please," she said. "I'll die if you're not inside me in the next two seconds."

Her begging scrambled his brain, the throb of her voice doubling the ache in his cock. The time for talking was over, unless it was *please, yes, more.* He hauled her up his body, urging her strong curved legs to part for his hips. She rubbed her breasts from side to side on his light chest hair. Her face was against his throat, her breaths panting. He set his jaw to make himself remember what they both needed. As he strode with her to the curtained bed, his shaft throbbed against the cleft of her tight bottom.

It felt hard enough to hold her up by itself.

"Please," she said again, squirming desperately. "Hurry."

Her sex flowed with wetness, painting his tense stomach. Groaning at the arousal that stabbed through him, he tumbled them with very little grace onto the mattress. Graceless or not, his mouth still found hers as his hand cupped her pubis hard. She was so wet she squelched when his grip contracted. Violet arched into his hold, clearly loving how his thumb dug through her delicate folds to work her swollen pearl up and down.

"Don't do that," she gasped even as her body thrashed in encouragement. "I want you . . . inside me . . . when I come."

His body moved before his thoughts could catch up. He was over her, panting, kneeing her thighs hastily apart. Her hand wrapped the part of him that hung, thick and shuddering and crazed, nearly parallel to his belly. Her thumb rubbed the generous precum around the head. Pleasure as sharp as sparks from a flint shot along his nerves.

"Yes," she crooned. "Give me *this.*"

He pulled her hand away, dragging it and its partner beside her head. The pillow and her gorgeous spill of hair cushioned the fists they made together. His tip nudged between her folds, not yet lined up at her gate. He tilted his pelvis the few degrees it needed for the blunt head to stopper her. The heat that welled around him drew his balls into knots.

"Violet," he warned, wracked by such unholy lust he could hardly speak through clenched teeth. "I'm the . . . only man who ever . . . is going to give you *this*."

Her eyes went wide a second before he shoved. He couldn't hold back. He had to claim her completely or lose his mind. She let out a soft cry of shock as her maidenhead rent for him. Even then he kept going, pushing and pushing until he was seated balls-deep inside of her. His neck arched with pleasure, knowing he'd hurt her but helpless not to feel good. The tight lush clasp of her around him surely had to be heaven.

"Good Lord," she gasped a bit unsurely.

His lungs heaved in and out like a cantering stallion's. He needed to move, to plunge in and out with the rut that was driving him. He'd spill oceans inside her pussy. He'd fuck her and fuck her until she screamed with pleasure.

Wait, he ordered his twitching body. *Wait until she's ready.*

She held his hands very tightly, their fingers wound together. He'd bowed his head, overwhelmed by the bliss of being inside her. Now he lifted it to look at her.

She was very flushed, her lips softly swollen from his kisses. Tiny sparkles of perspiration shone on her brow in the candlelight. He had an inkling not all of them were from pain.

"Augustin," she said, her pupils nearly swallowing her irises. "I can feel your pulse beating in my quim."

He had to smile at her wonder, to kiss the two cinnamon freckles on the tip of her nose. "I feel yours too, sweetheart."

She wriggled, just a little, and nearly took his head off with ecstasy. "I think I'd like you to move now."

He moved, and gasped, and then they both were slamming wildly into each other. This had to be the sweetest drug ever invented. The sex became a battle, each of them needing it so much. She was bruising him with her hips, and he'd never felt anything so wonderful. He had to tear their hands apart so they could hug each other, so they wouldn't thrust so desperately in and out that her pussy disengaged from his prick. That would have been intolerable, as unthinkable as not bringing every ounce of strength to bear on fucking each other.

They rolled—him on top, then her—grunting like maddened animals. He loved watching her ride him, his hands greedy on her breasts, her nipples tight hot stones.

"I can't come," she moaned, her hips swiveling and thumping.

"Oh God, but it feels so good."

He shifted his angle, trying to find the spot, the friction that would push them both over. It didn't seem to exist right then, though the pleasure of pumping into her boggled in its intensity. Adoring it as much as she did, he dug his fingers into her slamming hips.

"You," she panted. "You on top. You're stronger than I am."

He rolled her before she finished asking, pushing her beneath him to do the work they fervently needed. They lay sideways along the foot of the bed, ropes creaking wildly with every thrust. Violet's hand slapped up to grip one turned mahogany post, to keep his extremely determined thrusts from skidding both of them off the edge.

"Ah," she cried as he took advantage of the new position to go faster. "Yes . . . yes . . . *Augustin!*"

The muscles of her sheath clamped down as she screamed his name. His mouth stretched to scream as well, but all that came was a gasp for air. His balls were trying to turn inside out. Completely out of control, he shoved as deeply into her as he could. His orgasm erupted. As it did, his voice unlocked on a moan, the relief so welcome it was painful. The oceans came, jetting into her, forever marking her as his. Violet sagged beneath him while he spumed, hands gently petting back his hair.

"I can't stop," he whispered against her ear. It was true. His cock was one raw nerve from his climax, but his hips wouldn't stop moving. He needed more. He needed her.

Her hands slid down his sweating back to his rear. When she squeezed its muscles, he hardened up all the way again. Feeling this, she nipped his earlobe.

"Don't stop," she whispered as hot as fire.

He groaned and rolled her on top of him.

She smiled down at him, both hands braced on his shoulders, hair spread like a scarlet tent around them. It should have tangled or caught beneath him, but perhaps their joining had awoken new magic gifts. She certainly was resilient. He didn't seem to have hurt her any more than she'd hurt him. That realization made him want to groan louder yet. If he couldn't hurt her, this delirium never had to end. Her breasts swayed as she rode him, her motions gentler now but no less wonderful.

"I love you," she said, arching down to kiss him.

He slid his hands up her front, caressing those beautiful silken hills. With the tip of each index finger, he circled her cherry-ripe nipples. The peaks were so sensitized she twitched and creamed at the light pressure.

When he spoke, his voice was as thick as smoke. "I notice you didn't ask Bojik to remove your curse."

"I notice you didn't remind me to."

He sat up so that she was riding him from his lap. "Maybe I secretly hoped we'd end up here."

She wagged her brows at him. "Maybe I did as well."

Happiness suffused him at her teasing, the emotion so sharp and pure he knew that if he never felt it again, he'd always remember it. In every way she was prepared to be his equal, though at the time she'd parted from Bojik, she hadn't known Augustin would stay. Then and there, he made himself a promise. For her, he would learn to love—not by halves, not in spite of his broken state, but as completely as any human being ever had. In that moment, he couldn't doubt he'd be true to her. She was the other half of his soul.

With the decision, the oddest sensation unfolded inside his chest. It began as a softer version of the wrenching he'd experienced earlier. It reached its culmination as the center of his being just seemed to open up. From the place that had once been empty, warmth rushed out in a sunburst. The sensation was so intense the rays should have visible.

"Why do you look like that?" Violet asked, touching the side of his face.

Augustin wrapped his arms around her. "I love you," he said.

She laughed at his marveling tone, dropping little fairy kisses across his cheeks. To his delight, she groaned when his next thrust probed farther into her.

"Want to go faster?" he offered.

"Oh yes," she agreed throatily.

They gave in joyously to the madness, coming shortly after with matching moans. Profound though the pleasure was, Augustin's appetite lived on.

*

Violet felt like Eve with him hard and thick inside her, as if all the power in the world was hers. She could not mind that he hadn't softened.

She was soft enough for them both.

"Sorry," he said, fingers kneading the bruises he'd already put on her hips.

Violet didn't mind them either. The slight pain felt good to her. Apparently Bojik's curse gave her a strength to match her desires. She stroked his hands with hers, then slid a caress through the fine gold hairs on his forearms to the bends of his elbows. He shivered, the little tremor running up his cock into her. She creamed around it, his excitement wonderfully catching.

"I'm not sorry," she whispered.

His look turned smoldering, blue fire glinting as his hands slid to where his hardness went into her. Slowly, gently, his thumbs stroked the place their flesh became one. His thickness twitched inside her.

"Do you like that?" she asked. "Do you like seeing yourself take me?"

He nodded and, oh, she loved seeing him at the point where he couldn't speak, loved how the blood washed into his face and his breath came more shallowly. She moved her hands behind her, gripping him just above the knee. He tensed, but she knew it was with anticipation.

"I think I can give you a better view."

She lifted off him in a long tease, not all the way, just until the flaring rim of the head caught where she was tightest. The length of his shaft emerged from her body, his spent seed running out of her and down him. Violet liked watching that. Those blue pulsing rivers quickened more than her heartbeat. His thumbs rode up his veins to touch her. She pushed down and shuddered at the feel of him gliding in. He filled her enough to stretch.

"Again," he rasped. "I want to see that again."

She obliged him and herself, leaning farther back and tightening to give him more pressure.

"Again," he said, his voice darker.

She sank down and rose even slower than before.

"Christ," he breathed. "You're creaming down me. I'm going to lose my mind."

To her surprise, he lifted her off him, pushing her back onto the blankets and pulling her knees apart. "I *have* to do this," he said as he bent forward.

She moaned, because he'd burrowed straight into the wetness

between her folds and was making soft rooting sounds. Violet didn't think she'd ever felt anything so wicked as him sucking their mingled tastes off of her. His tongue probed deep, hands gripping her thighs to keep her open, controlling her as she arched. When he pulled her engorged clitoris into his mouth, when he rolled it against his tongue and pressed the slightest edge of his teeth to it, she came in a long spasm.

His laugh vibrated into her pussy right before he sat up. She hadn't heard him laugh like that before, so easily and open.

"You think that's funny?" she panted. "That you can make me come so quickly?"

His eyes were dancing, but his breath caught in the middle of his next chuckle. She was bending toward him, and he guessed what she meant to do.

Or at least part of it.

"Do it," he urged, backside resting on his heels. "Suck your taste off me."

Nothing loath, she took the silky head of him in her mouth. She could tell he liked that. As she sank, he jerked his knees wider. His hands came up to her head, gentle but tense as he guided her. She could tell he was fighting not to shove in too hard. The sprawl of his thighs gave her access to his balls, an invitation she was too sensual to refuse.

"Yes," he hissed as she cupped his sac. "Violet, that feels so good."

His testicles were tight and hot—no doubt tender from having come so hard. She let her hand baby them. The lightest taps set them swinging, the softest brushes raising thrill bumps along their skin. She stroked the firmness behind them but did not push. Sweetness began to seep from his tip: not seed but tears of new longing.

He gasped as she licked them, pressing more strongly between her lips.

She pulled back, raising one finger to keep him from following. His eyes tracked her motions as she gathered her outspilled hair. The ends formed a tail she dragged slowly across one palm, like a big painter's brush. Augustin's powerful thighs quivered.

"You'll enjoy this," she said. "It's like being stroked with feathers."

He made a little sound in his throat, repeating it as she pulled her gathered hair up his rigid prick. More beads welled from the slit, more goose bumps, more tremors he couldn't seem to control. She brushed the fan of red to his nipples, tickling the darkened tips. The prince's hands curled into white-knuckled fists. She sensed she'd pushed him right to the edge.

Because she wanted him to go over, she feathered her hair across his cockhead.

"Fuck," he hissed between clenched teeth.

Violet leaned in to lick his chin. "I only tease you because I love you so much."

That snapped through his control. He growled and grabbed her, turning and flinging her so she lay face down. Her heart thumped with excitement as he kneed her legs apart from behind.

Apparently, she'd been teasing a tiger.

"Fuck," he repeated, shoving one arm underneath her stomach to hitch her pelvis up. "You make me want you worse than ever."

He seemed bent on proving it. His cock jabbed toward her pussy, missing once before shoving solidly in. Pleasure blinded her as he filled her. She cried out and pushed back at him. Her name tore from him, the frenzy that overtook them just as raw as when he first penetrated her.

"*This*," he snarled as he humped at her. "This is what I wanted back at the brook. To fuck you. To fuck and fuck my cock in your sweet pussy."

He was babbling, every slamming thrust both punishment and reward. He slapped one palm to the rattling headboard, his second wrapped tight around her pubis. She loved when he did that, how his big hand swallowed her sex in safety, how he squeezed and massaged her from every side, remembering her no matter how deep his abandon was.

"Please," she begged, trying to push back harder. "Please make me go over."

"Oh God." His cock was swelling, his thrusts so quick he was only pulling out halfway. She arched, canting her hips to put the greatest pressure on the sweet spot beneath his head. He gasped, battering her with the smooth blunt tip. The pummeling felt so good on that tender wall, aching good, swooning good, the angle so perfect she was almost afraid to move. With all her strength, she tightened her sheath on him.

"*Violet*," her lover moaned.

Then he just screamed for her. His cock let loose a torrent of heat that flooded her deep inside. The sound, the feel, propelled her straight into ecstasy, teaching her the muscles of her pussy were a good deal mightier than she'd known. The orgasm was so forceful it dizzied her. She surrendered and flew, letting her body do what it would. Augustin groaned at the new milking of his shaft.

For just a second, she thought she might have blacked out.

When her senses recovered, Augustin's entire weight was squashing her to the bed.

He groaned again when she squeaked in protest but rolled off her. Neither of them could speak. They were too busy gasping for air. Violet did find the strength to wriggle around and hug him. With a grunt that could not have been more endearing, he dragged her on top of him. He was wonderfully warm and sweaty, the rise and fall of his chest as soothing as a boat rocking on small waves. Violet didn't think she could have been this purely relieved even if she'd never been cursed.

"That's it then," he slurred sleepily.

Violet lifted her cheek an inch. His eyes were half closed, his expression extremely smug. "That's it?"

"Yes, you've had your merry way with me. Now you must make me an honest man."

Violet returned her head to his chest and smiled. His hand was tangled possessively in her hair. Beneath her cheek, his supposedly faulty heart was pounding as vital and strong as hers. She harbored none of the doubts he had in himself. Her prince would love her better and truer than any princess was loved before. He'd come to like her people, and assuredly they'd love him. Arnwall would be better for his hand steadying hers. One day, perhaps, both their kingdoms would join. She patted the sturdy beating within his ribs. A soft sigh of happiness trailed from them in unison.

"I meant you have to marry me," he said, in case she hadn't figured it out.

Violet laughed silently to herself.

"As you wish, your highness," she said aloud.

◆ ◆ ◆

Werewolf cop Adam swears to protect and serve all the supernatural creatures in Resurrection, but he also watches out for unsuspecting human Talents who wander in from Outside.

Telekinetic Ari is just such a wanderer. She's tracking a crime boss who wants to exploit her gift for his own evil ends—a mission that puts her on a collision course with the hottest cop in the RPD.

Adam wants the crime boss too, but mostly he wants Ari. She's the mate he's yearned for all his life. Problem is getting a former street kid into bed with the Law could be his toughest case to date.

"*Hidden Talents* is the perfect package of supes, romance, mystery and HEA!" —**paperbackdolls.com**

*

CHAPTER 1

D usk settled over the city of Resurrection like a blanket of bad news.

That's me, Ari thought, flexing her right fist beside her hip. *Bad news with a capital B.*

This wasn't just whistling in the dark. Ari had been bad news to some people in her life. To her parents. To every teacher she'd had in high school. *You'll come to no good*, they'd threatened, and she couldn't swear they'd been wrong. Certainly, she hadn't turned out to be a blessing to Maxwell or Sarah. Because of her, Max was in the hospital with too many broken bones in his arms to count, and Sarah was God knew where. But at least Ari was trying to change that. At least she was trying to be bad news to people who deserved it.

To her dismay, Resurrection, NY wasn't what she'd been led to believe when she'd looked it up on the internet.

She stood on the crest of a weedy hill outside the metropolis, her presence hidden by the deeper shadow of a highway overpass. She'd been expecting a down-on-its-luck backwater. Storefronts stuck in the seventies. Maybe a real town square and a civil war battlefield. Instead, she found an actual cityscape. The skyline wasn't Manhattan tall, more like Kansas City. Few buildings looked brand new, but many were substantial. They formed a grid of streets and parkland whose core had to encompass at least five miles. This was definitely more than a backwater. Resurrection reminded her of city photos from the early decades of the last century, when *skyscraper* meant something exciting. What could have been a twin to the Chrysler Building stuck up from the center of downtown, reigning over its brethren.

Finding the Eunuch among all that was going to take some doing.

You have to find him, she told her sinking stomach. If she didn't, she and her very small gang of peeps would be looking over their shoulders for the rest of their lives. At twenty-six and thankfully still counting, Ari had endured more than enough hiding. She was stronger now. She'd been *practicing*. Henry Blackwater, aka, the Eunuch, wouldn't know what hit him.

"Right," she said sarcastically to herself. She'd be lucky if she got out of here alive.

But faint heart never vanquished fair villain. Ari knew she'd been born the way she was for a reason. Maybe here, maybe soon, she'd find out what that reason was.

CHAPTER 2

No one messed with people who belonged to Adam Santini. Unless, of course, the person messing with the person was also Adam's relative.

"You. Ate. My. Beignets." To emphasize his point, Adam's irate cousin, Tony Lupone, was bashing his brother's head against the squad room floor.

Since Rick's skull was made of sterner stuff than the linoleum, he laughed between winces. "What sort of cop—*ow*—eats beignets any-way?"

"Your faggot brother cop, that's who. Your pink-shirted faggot brother cop who's whupping your butt right now."

Amused by their exchange, Adam leaned back against Tony's cluttered desk. The precinct's squad room was a semi-bunker in the basement. A mix of ancient file cabinets and desks were balanced by some very revved-up technology. Grimy electrum grates on the windows protected them, more or less, from things that went bump in the night outside. The hodgepodge suited the men who manned it better than most workplaces could. Rough-edged but smart was the werewolf way. At the moment, Tony was so rough-edged his eyes glowed amber in his flushed face. His big brother could have defended himself better than he was, if it weren't for his rule against hitting his siblings.

"Ow! Lou!" he complained to Adam. "You're supposed to be my best friend. Aren't you going to call off this squirt?"

"You're the one who ate his fancy donuts."

"All dozen of them!" Tony snarled, his grievance renewed. "I brought them in to share."

"Shit," said longhaired Nate Rivera, Adam's other cousin, once removed. "Now *I* want to whup you."

Considering even-tempered Nate was growling, Adam judged it time to end the wrestling match. "All right, you two. Enough. Rick, I'm docking your next paycheck for the price of his beignets. Dana, if you'd be so kind, raid the coffee fund and pick up another batch for tomorrow night."

"None of which you're going to enjoy, Mister Pig!" Panting from the exertion of trying to give his brother a concussion, Tony rose and pointed angrily down at him. "You can choke on your damned donuts."

Wisely, Rick remained where he was while his little brother stalked back to the break room, where his heinous crime had been discovered. The dress code for the detectives was casual. Rick's gray RPD T-shirt was rucked way up his six-pack abs. His concave stomach didn't betray his gluttony. His fast werewolf metabolism saw to that.

"My head," Rick moaned, still laughing. "Come on, cuz. Give your beta a hand up."

Adam sighed and obliged. None of his wolves were small, but Rick was six four and all muscle. Even with supe strength, Adam grunted to haul him up. "Some second you are. You had to know this would cause trouble."

"I couldn't help myself. The box smelled so good. Plus, he was totally obnoxious about bringing them in for everyone."

"So you knew you were stealing food from my mouth?" Nate interjected, not looking up from his paperwork. "Not cool."

"He's sucking up. Ever since he came out, he's been—" Rick snapped his muzzle shut, but it was too late.

"Uh-huh," Nate said in his dry laid-back way. He'd spun around in his squeaky rolling chair to face Rick. "Ever since he came out, your brother stopped being a butch-ass prick. In fact, ever since he came out, he's been the nicest wolf around here. You don't like that 'cause you're used to being everyone's favorite."

"Crap." The way Rick rubbed the back of his neck said he knew he was in the wrong. Being Rick, he couldn't stay dejected long. A grin flashed across his handsome olive-skinned face. "Can't I still be everyone's favorite? Do I have to turn gay too?"

"I don't know," Nate said, returning to his work. "So far only gay boys bring us good breakfasts."

Seeing Rick's private wince, Adam patted his back and rubbed. Touchy-feely creatures that werewolves were, the contact calmed both of them. He knew Rick was still working on accepting his little brother's big announcement. Werewolves were some of the most macho supes in Resurrection, a city that had plenty to choose from. Adam knew Rick loved his brother just as much as before. He suspected Rick was mostly worried Tony would end up hurt. Being responsible for policing America's only supernatural-friendly town made the wolves enough of a target. Turning out to be gay on top of that was as good as taping a target onto your back.

"Tony will be all right," Adam assured his friend. "Everyone here is adjusting to the new him."

Rick rubbed his neck once more and let his hand drop. Worry pinched his dark gold eyes when they met Adam's. "They're pack. They have to love him."

Adam didn't believe this but wasn't in the mood to argue. Plenty of folks endowed being pack with mystical benefits. Some were real of course, but as alpha, Adam wasn't comfortable relying on magic to cement his authority. He thought it best to actually *be* a competent leader.

"Boss," Dana their dispatcher said. The young woman had her own corner of the squad room. Apart from its cubby walls, it was open. Banks of sleek computers surrounded her, each one monitoring different sectors of the city. The sole member of the squad who wasn't a relative, Dana was the most superstitious wolf Adam had ever met. Anti-hex graffiti scrawled across her work surfaces, the warding so thick he couldn't tell one symbol from another. How they worked like that was beyond him. Despite the quirk, Adam took her instincts seriously. Right then, she didn't look happy. Her silver dreamcatcher earrings were trembling.

"Boss, we've got a suspected M without L in the abandoned tire store on Twenty-Fourth."

M without L referred to the use of magic without a license. Adam's hackles rose. Jesus, he hated those. "Who's reporting the incident?"

"Gargoyle on the Hampton House Hotel." She touched her headset and listened. "He says it's a Level Four."

Adrenaline surged inside him, making his palms tingle. Gargoyles were rarely wrong about magical infractions. While the strength levels went up to eight, four was nothing to sneeze at. Thumb and finger to his mouth, Adam blew a piercing whistle to get his men's attention.

"Suit up," he said. "We've got a probable ML on Twenty-Fourth."

"Don't forget your earpieces," Dana added. "I'll help coordinate from here."

Adam's men were already loping to the weapons room. "Load for bear," he said as he followed them. "We don't know what we're in for."

*

Resurrection, New York couldn't have existed without the fae. For nearly two hundred years, it had sat on an outfolded pocket of the fae's other-dimensional homeland, *in* the human world but only visible to a special few.

Those who wandered in from Outside found it less alien than might be expected. The founding faeries had used the Manhattan of the 1800s as their architectural crib sheet. Since then, the bigger apple had continued to provide inspiration. Immigrants especially liked to recreate pieces of their native land. Resurrection had its own Fifth Avenue and Macy's, its own subway and museums. Little Italy still flourished here, though—sadly—its theater district was as moribund as its role model. Adam was familiar with the theories that Resurrection was an experiment, created to see if human and fae could live peaceably as in days of old. Whether this was the reason for its existence, he couldn't say.

The only fae he knew were exceptionally tight-lipped.

Whatever their motives, Resurrection had become a haven for humans with a trait or two extra. Shapechangers of every ilk thrived here. Vamps were tolerated as long as they behaved themselves. The same was true of demons and other Dims: visitors from alternate dimensions who entered through the portals. If a being could get along, it could stay. If it couldn't, it had to go. And if the visitors didn't want to go, Adam and the rest of the RPD were just the folks to make sure they went anyway.

The job fit Adam better than his combat boots, and those boots fit him pretty good. He loved keeping order, protecting the vulnerable, kicking butt and cracking skulls as required. The only duty he didn't like was apprehending rogue Talents. Sorcerers were trained at least, and demons who went dark side were generally predictable. Talents were the wild cards in an already dangerous deck. Their power was raw, depending not on spells but on how much energy they could channel. That amount could be a trickle or a mother-effing hell of a lot.

The previous year, a Level Seven Talent who'd gotten stoned on faerie-laced angel dust had taken down the six-lane Washington Street Bridge. Just popped it off its piers and let it drop in the North River. If the bridge's gargoyles hadn't swooped in to save what cars they could, the loss of life would have been astronomical. Adam still had nightmares about talking the tripping Talent into surrendering. If tonight's incident ran along similar lines, he might need a vacation.

Along with the rest of his team, Adam clutched the leather sway-strap above his head. Nate was driving the black response van because no one else dared claim the wheel from the ponytailed Latino. They all wore body armor and helmets, plus an assortment of protective charms. Their rifles leaned against the long side benches between their knees. The guns could fire a range of ammo, both conventional and spelled. Rick, who had a knack for effective prayer, was quietly calling on the precinct's personal guardian angel. Sometimes this worked and sometimes it didn't, but even the atheists among them figured better safe than sorry.

"God," Tony said, tapping the back of his head against the van's rattling wall. "I hope this isn't another thing like the bridge."

"Amen," Carmine agreed. The stocky were was the oldest member of their squad, the only one who was married, and—yes—another of Adam's cousins.

Before he could smile, Adam's earpiece beeped.

"You're four blocks out," Dana said. "The gargoyle is reporting another series of power flares. Still nothing higher than a Four."

That was good news. Unless, of course, the Talent was warming up.

"Okay, people," Adam said. "Watch your tempers once we get inside. Be safe but no killing unless you have no choice."

He didn't warn them against hesitating. Given their inbred hair-trigger werewolf nature, hesitating wasn't an issue.

*

The defunct tire store sat on a small parking lot between a very well locked print shop and a transient hotel. Apart from the hotel, which wasn't exactly bustling, the area wasn't residential. A cheap liquor outlet on the corner drew a few customers, but the main business done here after dark was drugs. Most of the product filtered in from the human world. Since this was Resurrection, some was also exotic. If you knew who to ask, you could score adulterated vamp blood or coke cut with faerie dust. Demon manufactured Get-Hard was popular, though it tended to cause more harmful side effects than Viagra. Every EMT Adam knew had asked why they couldn't get GH off the street. All Adam could answer was that they were doing the best they could.

Policing Resurrection couldn't be about stamping out Evil. It had to be about making sure Good didn't get swallowed.

The reminder braced him as he and his team ran soundlessly from the van onto the buckled and trash-strewn asphalt of the parking lot. His scalp prickled half a second before a soft gold light flared around the edges of the boarded-up back windows.

Adam had answered previous calls to this location. The rear section of the tire store was where vehicles had been cranked up on lifts for servicing. Fortunately, there was plenty of cover for slipping in. Unfortunately, lots of flammables were inside. Adam took the anti-burn charm that hung around his neck and whispered a word to it. That precaution seen to, he hand-signaled Rick and Tony to split off and block escape from the front exit.

This left Adam, Carmine and Nate to ghost in the back.

The flimsy combination lock on the door to the service bay had been snapped—probably magically. Adam and his two detectives ducked under the low opening. Inside, the scent and feel of magic was much stronger, the air thicker and hotter than it should have been in autumn. A male voice moaned in pain farther in, standing Adam's hair on end. Without needing to be told, Nate peeled off to the right. Adam and Carmine took the left.

Scattered heaps of tires allowed them to creep up on their goal without being seen. One bare bulb dangled from a wire, lighting the far end of the garage. In the dim circle beneath it, the Talent had her moaning victim tied to a plastic chair. The sight of her stopped Adam in his tracks. Christ, she was little. Five foot nothing and probably a hundred and small change. She looked to be in her twenties and wore the kind of clothes street kids did. Ripped up black jeans. Ancient T-shirts that didn't fit. Her oversized Yankees jacket had its sleeves torn out and was decorated with unidentifiable small objects. Her hair was a shade of platinum not found in nature, standing in white spikes around her head. A swirling red pattern was dyed it, as if her coiffure were her personal art project. What really got him though, what had his breath catching in his throat, was the clean-cut innocence of her face. Outfit and hair aside, she looked like a tiny Iowa farm girl.

It made his chest hurt to look at her. The part of him that needed to protect others wanted to protect her.

Knowing better than to trust in appearances, Adam shook the inclination off. He tapped the speaker fixed into his vest with the signal for everyone to hold. The victim was still alive. They could afford to take a minute to discover what they were up against.

As they watched, the girl lifted her right hand. Pale blue fire outlined her curled fingers. Her already bloodied victim shrank back within his ropes. He was some kind of elf-human mixblood with long gray hair. He was a lot bigger than the Talent, but that didn't mean their fight had been fair. Despite the elf blood, he didn't give off much of a magic vibe. A near null was Adam's guess. His run-in with the Talent had left damage. He looked bad: eyes swollen, bruises, shallow cuts bleeding all over. Though he seemed familiar, as injured as he was, he was hard to identify. Even his smell was distorted by blood and fear.

"I can do this all night," the Talent said in a voice that was way too sweet for a torturer. "Or you can tell me where to find the Eunuch."

Carmine and Adam came alert at that. This was a name they knew too damn well.

"Lady," said her bloodied victim. "I have no idea who you mean."

The girl closed her glowing hand gently. The man she was interrogating arched so violently he and the plastic chair fell over. He screamed as blood sprayed from a brand-new cut on his chest.

Carmine started forward, but Adam gripped his shoulder.

"Wait," he murmured. "That cut was shallow. He's not in immediate danger."

Carmine shook his head but obeyed. When the man stopped writhing, the girl drew a deep slow breath. With no more effort than gesturing upward with one finger, she set man and chair upright. Despite the situation's danger, something inside Adam let out an admiring *whoa*.

"Clearly," she said, "you think you ought to be more afraid of your boss than me."

"Lady," panted the injured man, "*everyone's* more afraid of him."

The girl's lips curved in a smile that had Carmine shivering beside him. Admittedly, the expression was a little scary. For no good reason Adam could think of, it made his cock twitch in his jockstrap.

The Talent spoke silkily. "I'm glad we've established you know who I'm looking for."

Adam expected her to cut him again. Instead, discovering her victim did know the Eunuch inspired her to up the ante on her torture. The blue fire she'd called to her hand now began gleaming around her feet. She was drawing energy from the earth—and no piddling amount either. Her glowing hand contracted into a fist, and her victim's face went chalky. Adam was pretty sure she was telekinetically squeezing his beating heart. Unless she was really good at medical manipulation, she was going to kill him.

"*Go*," he said sharply into his vest microphone.

Even in human form, werewolves weren't slowpokes. What went down next was textbook perfect. Adam and his men were on the Talent so fast she didn't have a chance to shift her attack to them. Nate got her nose squashed down on the oil-stained floor, then snapped electrum plated cuffs snug around her wrists. The cuffs were charmed so she couldn't break them, no matter how powerful she was. The Talent struggled, then cried out as Nate yanked her roughly onto her feet.

He dropped a depowering charm around her neck for good measure. Immediately, the energy-charged air settled back to normal. The girl gaped at the enchanted medal, then straight up at Adam. Adam's heart stuttered in his chest. Her eyes were a breathtaking corn-fed blue, her lashes a thick dark brown. The twitch she'd sent through his cock morphed into a throb. Carmine shot him a look of surprise. Adam fought an embarrassed flush. The smell of his arousal must have gotten strong enough to seep through his clothes.

"'bout time you showed up," the girl's victim huffed. "This bitch needs to be locked up."

Carmine flipped up his face shield and turned to consider him. The man flinched back, obviously wishing he'd refrained from complaining.

"Aren't you Donnie West?" Carmine asked. "'Cause I know we've got a handful of outstandings on your drug dealing ass."

"Uh," said Donnie, abruptly recognizable under his bruises.

"That's what I thought," said Carmine, and let out his belly laugh.

Through all of this, the Talent's eyes moved from one of them to the other, taking in their gear and their guns and getting wider by the second. When Rick and Tony caught up to them from the front, Tony's upper canines had run out and his amber eyes were glowing. The girl sucked in a breath like this shocked her, though a partial change when younger wolves got excited wasn't uncommon.

"What the—" she said before having to swallow. "What the hell kind of cops are you?"

Still holding her from behind, Nate's slash of a mouth slanted up in a devilish grin. "Well, what do you know," he drawled. "Looks like we've got ourselves an Accidental Tourist."

The Hidden Series is available in ebook and print.

About the Author

E mma Holly is the award winning, *USA Today* bestselling author of more than forty romantic books featuring billionaires, genies, faeries and just plain extraordinary folks. She loves the hot stuff, both to read and to write!

If you'd like to discover what else she's written, please visit her website at www.emmaholly.com.

Emma runs monthly contests and sends out newsletters that often include notice of special sales. To receive them, go to her contest page.

Thanks so much for reading this book. If you enjoyed it, please consider leaving a review. That kind of support is very helpful!

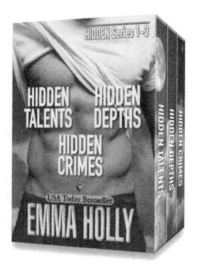

Three full-length paranormal romances: *Hidden Talents*, *Hidden Depths* and *Hidden Crimes*. Whether they're irresistible werewolf cops, sexy wereseal kings, or sassy firefighting tigresses, these supernatural heroes turn up the heat!

Books 1 – 3 in the Hidden Series

"The perfect package of supes, romance, mystery and HEA!"
—**Paperback Dolls** on *Hidden Talents*

"You will fall head over heels [with] the amazingly sensuous and intensely graphic world . . . One of the best erotic romances I have ever read."
—**BittenByLove** on *Hidden Depths*

"If you are looking for suspense, passion and a touch of the paranormal, don't look any farther than *Hidden Crimes*."—**Joyfully Reviewed**

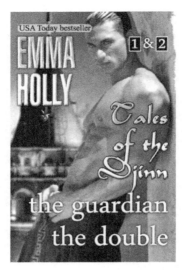

When a mysterious stranger with a briefcase full of cash moves into Elyse's brownstone, she never imagines he's a genie. Cade is gorgeous and sophisticated, but nothing about him adds up . . . that is, until she learns he's a magical being desperate to break a curse on his home city.

Teaming up with a human female isn't the only challenge Elyse's tenant will have to face. His trip to Elyse's world created a duplicate of himself, a not-quite carbon copy who believes *he's* Cade's superior.

Commander Arcadius should be easy for Elyse to resist. He's arrogant, insensitive, and a chauvinist—making it obvious he doesn't think much of her. Then, bit-by-bit, she sees past his prickly exterior. Arcadius is who Cade used to be before they met. If she fell for one man, chances are she'll fall for the other.

Two full-length novels of the Djinn

"FANTASTIC! [T]his may be the best thing she has written to date . . . an epic tale of romantic fantasy."—**In My Humble Opinion**

"Addictive . . . should not be missed!"—**Long and Short Reviews**

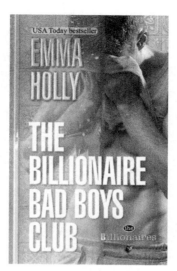

Self-made billionaires Zane and Trey have been a club of two since they were eighteen. They've done everything together: play football, fall in love, even get smacked around by their dads. The only thing they haven't tried is seducing the same woman. When they set their sights on sexy chef Rebecca, these bad boys meet their match!

"This book is a mesmerizing, beautiful
and oh-my-gods-hot work of art!"
—**BittenByLove** 5-hearts review

The man everybody wants

Women can't keep their hands off billionaire Damien. The mysterious mogul has it all: fast cars, killer looks, and a brain that just might be his best asset.

Mia loves her job at a PI firm. Her coworker Jake stars in most of her daydreams, so seeing him every day is no hardship.

Jake hasn't believed in human goodness since he worked black ops for the CIA. Romancing innocent Mia is unthinkable, no matter how enticingly submissive she seems to be. Then a case of corporate espionage forces them to pose as dom/sub duo, to catch the eye of accused wrongdoer Damien. No fantasy is off limits for this voyeur—until the attraction the pair exerts lures him to go hands on . . .

"I. love. this. ménage. I am still smiling about these characters. Another outstanding story."—**Mary's Ménage Reviews**

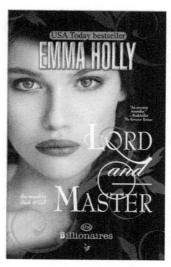

My name is Mia and I'm a lucky girl

Billionaire Damien didn't stop being moody just because Jake and I moved in with him. Fortunately, I've devised a strategy. I inherited a share in an exclusive erotic club, and they're beta testing a role-play game. Surrounded by period perfect detail, members pretend to be Edwardian lords and ladies . . . or stable masters, if they prefer.

By switching up our dynamic, I'm hoping to smooth the snags in our otherwise fabulous ménage. Neither of my lovers has trouble opening his heart to me, but Damien would benefit from exploring his dominant side, and he and Jake could be easier with each other.

That's my goal anyway. My plan might go up in smoke when Jake and Damien concoct their own scheme for me!

The sequel to *Beck & Call*

"So good it defies description . . .The entire premise of the book was fantastic . . . [L]ives up to and exceeds expectations."—Jean Smith, **x-treme-delusions**

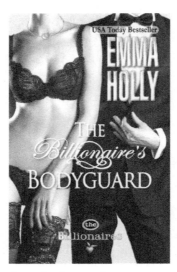

A.J. is as cynical as she is badass, a former cop turned bodyguard. A lifetime of hard knocks taught her not to trust—a handy trait in her line of work. Given the right motivation, she knows anyone will betray their near and dear. Rather than let them betray her, A.J. keeps her shields nailed up.

On the surface, Luke's life seems charmed. He's a Hollywood action hero whose looks inspire fantasies. Known for being easygoing and kind to fans, his latest film made him a billionaire producer. Problem is his high profile is attracting a dangerous class of admirer.

Threats like the one Luke faces aren't new. A.J. saved his life once already. Now he doesn't trust anyone but her to guard him. With a deadly enemy lurking in the shadows, this star-crossed pair better pray A.J.'s skills are sharp!

"A romance story fans of *The Bodyguard* will appreciate . . . a great read and an easy recommend."—Xeranthemum, **Long and Short Reviews**

(formerly published as *Star Crossed*)

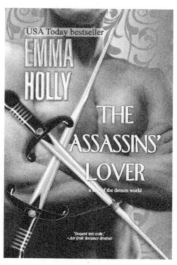

Assassin-guards Ciran and Hattori were bred to live by a code. Never betray your master and never lose your heart. Each icy man is all the other needs until they're sent to kill the beautiful demon princess, Katsu. Against all expectations, this tenderhearted female teaches them they can love. The trio's future would be sweet . . . but only if they escape the enemy who wants to slay them all!

A tale of an alternate Victorian world

"I feel as if I am actually friends with these characters . .
. groundbreaking . . . an absolute Must Read."
—You Gotta Read Reviews

"An erotic powerhouse that dives right into what readers love best
about the . . . amazing mind of Ms. Holly."
—Whipped Cream Reviews

Printed in Great Britain
by Amazon